RESURRECTION

by

David W. Adams

RESURRECTION

2

Also available from this author

The Dark Corner

To The Moon & Back

Return to the Dark Corner

Wealdstone

Little Nightmares : The Wrong Place

The Dark Corner : Complete Trilogy

RESURRECTION

4

For Nan & Grandad,

Marlene and Dave.

Thank you for all of your support, and love through everything life has thrown at me and Charlotte.

Nobody has greater grandparents than I do.

RESURRECTION

6

ONE

As Molly gazed down at the floor of the carriage, she couldn't help but think to herself, how she had clearly seen that exact piece of chewing gum and that Mars bar wrapper stuck to the same spot the day before. Rolling her eyes at the lack of cleanliness exhibited on public transport these days, she gazed out the window at the typical rain streaks. July in the UK. A guaranteed cycle of wind, torrential rain, and maybe an hour of sunshine every few days.

The weather did cause quite a beautiful spectacle though when it came to bodies of water. There was something raw and powerful about watching a river or the ocean churning up with the wind and the thunderstorms. Molly had always loved watching those nature programmes featuring the world's deadliest weather. She would often watch them on the journey to the base on her pad.

Today though, she was way too tired. The work on the new pulsar cannons was becoming more like a waking nightmare. The new energy based weapon being developed by the British Military had been a closely guarded secret, until one of their own decided to switch to the USAF, and reveal everything to the Americans. Now they were under pressure to get the prototypes up and working three years ahead of schedule. So much for the so-called Defence Coalition. Everybody was still out to beat down everybody else.

7

One-hundred-and-ten-thousand pounds a year salary, and Molly constantly thought to herself that perhaps it just wasn't worth it. She had been indoctrinated into the military by her father. He had not been a military man himself, but her mother had served in the British Army during the Third World War thirty years previously. She had won the highest military honour for a rescue mission which saved the life of seventy-two people, cut off by the Russians. She was then captured and executed one week before the ceasefire.

Molly, however, was against violence of all kinds, and agreed to join the military only on a research basis. She had spent six years trying to ignore the fact she was helping design and develop the very weapons she was against using, by convincing herself that she wasn't the one using them, and she was doing it in her mother's memory. But after seeing the initial testing, and watching a single blast from a handheld version of the weapon obliterate an entire disused factory in Plymouth, she was beginning to consider pulling out.

This was a thought that occurred to her daily. However, her thought process was interrupted by a vibration from her pocket. As she pulled out her phone, others on the bus reacted to their own alerts. The screen lit up with a notification from Sky News.

"World leaders issue emergency order instructing all individuals to remain indoors, or head for the nearest safe location following the arrival of unidentified craft into Earth's atmosphere."

Chatter began building around the train, as everyone tried to speculate what this meant. Molly got a sickening feeling in her stomach, as her eyes looked out of the carriage windows to scan the skies for this unknown craft. Even though she was almost certain this had nothing to do with her research, a part of her brain was concerned her weapon programme may have attracted unwanted attention. No contact from outside of Earth had ever formally been received, except a single signal fifteen years earlier which appeared to originate from the edge of the solar system, but was never confirmed or translated.

Panic began to set in amongst the passengers, as more notifications came up on people's phones. Molly's own chimed to a new piece of information.

"The Prime Minister instructs the British people to remain indoors, and contact their loved ones to ensure they follow the same guidance."

Molly then had an alert from her commanding officer.

"All staff, scientists, and officers are to report to their nearest military installation immediately using whatever means of transport available for an emergency summit."

By this point, the driver had brought the transport to a stop, and was now on the radio to his manager, and Molly headed for the front to speak to him.

"Hey, what's the situation?" she asked.

9

The driver replaced his radio and shook his head.

"Whatever this thing is, they want all transports back to the depot immediately, with all passengers for safety reasons."

Molly shook her head, and flashed her military identity card to him.

"The military has ordered all staff to use whatever transport is viable to head to the nearest base. Seeing as how I'm on your train, that's where we are all going. No safer place than an Army base right?"

The driver nodded in agreement. It was after all hard to argue with that. He handed Molly the tannoy, and allowed her to address the other passengers, who were now freaking out.

"Ladies and Gentlemen, may I please have your attention."

The train fell silent.

"Thank you. My name is Molly Coben, and I am a research scientist at the Defence Coalition. I have been instructed to head for the nearest base as soon as possible, where it is safe. As I'm travelling with you good people, that's where we are *all* heading. No safer place to be right now. Please don't panic, I'm sure everything will be…"

Molly was cut off by an immense noise of what sounded like thunder, and the carriages rocked violently. As she spun around, she saw two bolts of what looked to be pure energy hit the bridge in front of them, and begin spreading across the tracks towards them.

A low vibration began rumbling beneath the train, and as the passengers watched on in disbelief, the bridge simply disintegrated beneath them. As the railway vanished, the train lurched forwards, and as each person grabbed hold of a rail or seat, it plunged down towards the river below, along with all of the other vehicles that had been on the neighbouring road bridge.

The impact of the water smashed the windows immediately, sending Molly and the driver flying upwards, apparently defying gravity, before landing in the water which was now creeping up the vertically impacted vehicle. They both clambered up the seats, as the train began to sink. Dazed and confused, many of the passengers refused to move, others were simply screaming as the water rushed up to greet them. All around them, Molly could hear more impacts into the water, and between the streaks of rain, she could see buildings turning to dust, and random bursts of light from within the dark clouds. She grabbed the driver by the shoulder.

"We need to get the emergency exits open! Get these people out!"

The driver nodded and together, they climbed up the upturned seats like a ladder, constantly aware of the water climbing up behind them. As the driver kicked open the rear door to the first carriage, he and Molly helped launch as many people into the water as possible, before jumping into the water themselves. As she kicked her way to the surface, Molly just about saw the last part of the train sink below the waves, hands still clambering at the glass from those who hadn't made it out.

The waves battered the survivors, as the water swirled and rose around them. Each stride towards the shore was met with a backhand from a wave, sending them back into the deeper parts of the river. The current was in turmoil, first carrying them one way, and then seemingly reversing and dragging them back another. Through water battered eyes, Molly saw the entire city around her fall into ash, like it was made of burnt paper, and just before she fell below the waves, energy completely exhausted, she caught the outline of a vessel. An enormous dark ship emerging from the clouds. The rumble from the vessel's immense size vibrated even the water around her.

As the train driver vanished between the waves, and failed to return, Molly's own limbs gave up on her. The power of the water was simply too much. The final thing she saw was the ship heading upwards back through the clouds, and the river began to drop off the end of what was apparently a waterfall. The very planet itself was falling away.

Her vision blurred as the oxygen left her brain, and she thought she saw a blue haze of light break through the dark green mist of the water, but she couldn't focus on it. She stopped kicking against the current. It was no use. As she sank towards the darkest depths, the only thought running through her mind was that her weapon must be responsible.

And as her guilt began to consume her, so did the river.

T W O

The fiery orange flares from the surface of the sun pierced the absolute darkness of the space around it. The pure contrast of the two colours seemed to enhance the aura from the celestial body. The liquid surface raged like a fierce river, twisting and turning, swirling in patterns, each more unique than the last.

As it burned ever brighter, the light glinted off the surface of a twenty-one-fifty-five Ford F150 pickup, floating in the abyss… and the eyes of its former owner.

The debris was few and far between, but each piece told a story. The chunk of lush green meadow which had once belonged to the countryside of Austria, the blades of the grass scorched on their tips, but now frozen at their base. The fragments of rock that had once formed part of the Snowdonia mountain ranges in Wales. And the torch, jagged metal at its base, which had once stood so proud with its holder in New York City.

And then there were the people.

Thousands of people, floating aimlessly through the ocean of space. Mothers, still with the tears frozen in their eyes, floated past their children, hands still reaching out towards them. Students from universities and schools worldwide, deprived of living their full lives, never to see what the human race was to become.

The pieces of countries now gone forever, and the remains of seas and streams, and rivers now cascading through the weightlessness, with no destination.

The few precious minerals in the stranded sections of the destroyed planet were now also catching the light of the sun, and they reflected it across the field of decimation. Prisms and rainbows formed on the crystallized skin of the victims of Earth.

They had not been ready.

Nobody had been ready when the end came.

Except *them*.

They were ready. They had prepared for thousands of centuries to do what they had done. And Earth had just been a stepping stone on their checklist, and now it was job done, and on to the next planet.

As their ship pushed its way through the debris field, the navigational lights on the side of each engine pylon blinked alternately, as what used to be the home of over nine-billion people bounced off the hull, as if it were dust. Much of it now was.

The dull hum of the engines was like a growl. A rumble of thunder on a constant loop, dominating any other sound for light-years. The vessel itself was immense. Easily the size of what was formerly Australia, it lumbered through space, a great metal behemoth, bowing to nothing, and granting mercy to no-one. The ship was as

14

dark as the vacuum of space itself, the panels reflecting the environment around it.

But even though this battle was over, the overall task was not finished. As the floating pick-up truck was crushed under the nose of the ship, the engines began to throb louder, the vibrations causing the reflected imagery to visibly ripple. It tilted to the side as it began to pick up speed, heading out of the system. There were more humans out there. Ones that had ventured where they shouldn't have. And they too must be eliminated.

As the ship lurched forward beyond the speed of light, leaving a bright green flash behind it, the site of the planet Earth, now only occupied by dust and debris, fell silent once more.

Despite the death, and the destruction and complete evaporation of an entire civilisation, the imagery cast by the sun was simply stunning. Arcs of colour ranging from the brightest and warmest oranges, to the fiercest reds, and the most golden of yellows lit up the sky.

A second ship rippled into view near Venus, the planet now travelling towards Mercury, out of its orbit, and on course for destruction. This ship however, was different. Much smaller in size, and more streamlined in appearance. It had clearly waited for the aggressors to leave the system before revealing itself. Smaller and nimbler, the vessel was constructed of a blue and purple hull, the design swept back like a teardrop falling through the air. Behind the main body of the ship, were two large cylindrical engines, glowing

15

white as they came into life. A large window on the front of the ship gave a view of the situation, and the occupant at the controls surveyed what was before him.

He, himself, was quite a sight to behold. Standing eight feet tall, and composed mostly of a humanoid form, his skin was similar to that of a human, but tinged with a shade of teal, and atop his head was a mane of fine, long golden hair, and his eyes glowed violet.

However, as he took in the imagery through his main window, his hair transformed into a pitch black colour, and his eyes deepened in their purple hue, growing in intensity until his pupils had vanished completely. He was heartbroken, and his incredibly varied body parts were reflecting his sadness. Pressing several buttons on the control panel, he steered the ship away from the sun, and charted a course out of the system. Engaging the auto-pilot, he turned away and made no jolted movement as the ship hit the speeds of the other vessel. He left what appeared to be the bridge of the ship, and entered another room, which was lined wall to wall with cryogenic tubes.

Ice was frozen on the glass of each and every installation, and in each one stood a member of a different species. In the first was what appeared to be a gorilla, six feet tall, but with humanoid hands, and facial features, matched by hair long enough to rival the pilots. In another was clearly a reptilian species, the dark green scales standing out amongst the rooms light blue walls, and the purple edging of the tubes themselves.

But the pod that the pilot was focussing on was the final one on the right. As he approached it, he placed his enormous hand on the glass.

"I am sorry that I could not save more of you. But I will."

His words echoed around the empty chamber, but the reflection of the human being before him was locked in his violet eyes, which were now filled with tears. He had shed tears thousands of times, for each species that he had watched become another statistic on the list of recently extinguished life. As the first tear trickled down, he blinked it away, his lids closing diagonally from all four corners as opposed to horizontally. As he removed his hand from the glass, and headed back out of the room, the lights went down, and inside the pod as the cryogenic process began, the eyes of the human woman snapped open. As she placed her hand upon the glass, Molly's expression was frozen in place, and the door to the room was closed.

RESURRECTION

THREE

Two hundred years later

As he flew backwards through the air and felt his back smash into the liquor bottles on the shelves behind him, Jaxx knew that things were not going well for him. His fall to the floor was even worse, landing on several shards of the glass he had just broken. The fall was worth it though, for behind the bar was the late barkeep's weapon: a rather large Beresian disruptor.

"Now that's what I'm talking about!" he exclaimed as he reached for the weapon.

The air in the bar continued to be filled with the screams of the clientele and the sound of breaking furniture. And bones. Jaxx was never one to give in or take the easy route out of things. That's usually why he found himself being thrown into the air, and nursing dozens of wounds each week. He used to feel that his bulking mass was a deterrent against oncoming violence. And in fairness to him, he was an imposing figure to most species. Standing at around six-foot-nine, and easily weighing in as much as a pro wrestler on any planet, most people would simply avoid conflict.

Unfortunately, two things were wrong with that scenario. Number one was that Allurians were even bigger. And number two was that Jaxx's personality did not match his imposing physique. He was quite a different prospect to his appearance. And having had several run-ins with the Allurians, they knew this all too well.

"Where are you? Spineless piece of rectal sputum!" The Allurian leader bellowed, spittle spraying across the room.

Still trying to figure out why the disruptor wasn't powering on, Jaxx decided to take a leaf out of some old action movies he'd seen and stall with banter, whilst also checking on the condition of a small metal disc in his pocket. Good, it was still illuminated.

"Oh, I'm just trying to figure out if I wanna shoot you in the head first, and spare your suffering, or take out each limb and look you in the eyes before I pull the final trigger. Any preference?"

Rage was the way of life for the Allurians, and Jaxx had been warned about trying to do a business deal with these people on a number of occasions. He didn't have many friends in his line of work, but he had a few sources and contacts that he could trust. And none of them trusted the Allurians. But where there was money, Jaxx tended to follow his instincts.

"I will carve out your heart and adorn my wall with your skin!" The Allurian snarled.

Jaxx finally managed to coax the weapon into life, and as the bright yellow glow filled the power cell, he smiled.

"So, no preference then?"

He leapt up and spun around, launching a cascade of bright yellow energy bursts around the room, taking out three of his aggressors before the power cell went dark again. As he looked down at the weapon in frustration, and started banging it with his hand to try getting it to work again, the lead Allurian, Finbar, tore it from his grasp and with a vast display of strength, snapped the device in half, and threw it on the floor. Reaching over the bar, he grabbed Jaxx by the collar and hauled him towards him, spinning on the spot, and once again launching him through the air. This time, he landed backside first in the neon light that formed the 'Welcome' sign over the bar entrance.

"You were warned not to trifle with my people again or you would suffer the consequences. Give me back what is mine, or I will tear you apart limb from limb, and search your carcass for it!"

Jaxx slowly regained his composure enough to stand, nursing his back, and removing the small shards of material he could feel protruding. Allurians were strong, but not particularly fast, or smart.

"You know, for such a fearsome race, you sure do talk a lot."

The sarcasm did not do much to lower the levels of anger in Finbar, as he let out an animalistic roar. The vibrations from his footsteps rumbled through the entire bar as he lumbered towards Jaxx, who was waiting, bouncing on his tiptoes, and then as Finbar got within inches of him and leapt, Jaxx ducked to the right, allowing Finbar to launch himself into the wall, fracturing the metal with his enormous weight.

Jaxx made a run for the door, but he was blocked by the arrival of three more Allurians, the middle one giving him a swift kick to the ribs, and again he flew across the room, smashing through one of the remaining tables. As he landed, his head became distorted and his vision blurred. His white eyes began to lose a grip on his sight, and as he reached around to feel the back of his head, he felt the blood trickling down.

Seconds later, he felt the hot and sweaty breath of Finbar on his face, but couldn't quite summon the strength to move away, and he felt the paw-like hand of the beast searching his jacket, until it came upon the thing that he had been trying to protect.

Removing the transparent computer module from his possession, Finbar stood back and twirled it in his palm. A wry smile spread across his face, as he looked down at the crumpled man before him.

"I thought your people were meant to be strong, Valkor! But you are as brittle and fragile as an egg! Perhaps you are one of these *lesser species!*"

Jaxx didn't like being insulted. He remembered watching an old Earth transmission of *Back to the* Future when he was a child. And he, much like Marty McFly, was not a fan of having his bravery questioned. His eyes began to focus again, and he began to regain some strength.

"Tear this puny being apart, and then burn this place to the ground."

Finbar turned and moved to walk out of the room, but a final note of sarcastic wit penetrated his hardened skin much more effectively than the disruptor ever could have.

"Your wife didn't seem to think I was a lesser species."

As Finbar turned on the spot, he saw a now standing Jaxx holding what appeared to be a gold chain, hanging on which was a pendant displaying the Allurian symbol for love.

Finbar clenched his fists with such force, that he very nearly crushed the chip he had fought to retrieve, and he barrelled forwards, smashing the three others out of the way, and moving the fastest he had ever moved, charged down towards Jaxx, who was now clutching a snapped metal leg from the table he had landed on, hidden behind his back. He wasn't sure if the object would penetrate the skin of Finbar, but he had no tricks left. Finbar raised his fists high in the air, and as Jaxx went to swing the pipe forwards, six shots rang out through the air.

As each one penetrated Finbar's skin, he was knocked back, and the final bolt between his eyes knocked him to the floor. Jaxx spun around searching for the source of the mysterious firepower. As he did so, another three shots rang out, taking out each of the other Allurians instantly.

Spinning around, Jaxx could see nobody.

"What the hell?" he asked, but received no reply.

Behind him, he heard movement, and as he turned one of the earlier Allurians had decided to regain consciousness and charge him, but as he held his arms up in defence, another shot dispatched him too. This time, Jaxx spun around to see a cloaked figure in the entrance to the bar holding a type of rifle he hadn't seen for a very long time.

"Umm, thanks," he said, as he squinted his glowing white eyes to try and get a better look at the figure.

"Don't mention it," came the reply. "You know you really shouldn't mess with Allurians. They will literally eat you for breakfast."

"Yeah, so I've heard."

The figure stepped forwards, and in the flickering sparks from where the lights and sign used to be, Jaxx could make out the long hair of a woman protruding from beneath the hood of the coat.

"So are you really that stupid, or are you super clever with bad luck?" asked the hooded woman, as she holstered her weapon.

Edging forward slightly, still very much focussed on trying to identify his rescuer, Jaxx shrugged his shoulders.

"I like to think I'm more of the smart professor, crossed with a vigilante type deal. Occasionally a reputable businessman. You?"

The woman laughed, and as more flecks of light emerged onto her face, Jaxx stopped in his tracks. He held his hand to his mouth, and for the first time that night, he was speechless.

The woman noticed, and reached up to lower her hood, and confirm Jaxx's suspicions were correct.

"What's the matter, you've never seen a human before?" she offered.

The truth of the matter was that he hadn't. Not a real one, anyway. The woman was seemingly in her mid-twenties, long auburn hair, styled in waves down to her collarbone. Her skin was bright, but her eyes told a different story. They had seen battle, and the dark circles beneath them suggested sleeplessness. Her cloak was the real surprise though. Jaxx knew that material. He had traded it for good money once before, when he had been in a tight spot. It was from a Saxon Captain. A race which had been gone for over two centuries.

"How?" was all Jaxx could muster, despite his earlier bravado.

"I don't really have time for the whole, *how can you be alive* speech, so let's save it for later, yeah?"

The woman hit a couple of buttons on her rifle, drew it back out of her holster, aimed it at Jaxx, and despite his protests and raised hands, she fired a shot at his chest, and he fell backwards through the only remaining chair in the place, crushing it beneath him.

The woman moved across to Finbar's corpse, and pulled the module from his hands.

"I'll take that, thank you very much."

She placed it in her pocket, before moving over to Jaxx. Reaching into another pocket, she pulled out a long oblong strip of metal, and tossed it down onto his chest. She raised her arm to reveal a bracelet on her left wrist, and with the touch of a couple of buttons, a bright orange forcefield encompassed Jaxx in his unconscious state, and raised his body from the floor.

"The amount of times you fly through the air, you should be earning frequent flyer miles," she said as she led him via an invisible leash out of the bar.

She paused briefly, thinking she had heard movement. Waiting for a few seconds, she decided it was nothing, and as Molly left the bar, she towed Jaxx behind her.

One thing was for certain though, the encounter had not gone unnoticed. Once Molly had left, over in the corner of the bar, the sound of broken glass crunching underfoot echoed around the now silent establishment. A figure emerged, completely transparent with no discernible features, moving across the floor. He reached for his own bracelet device on his wrist, and following an initial beep, his true form materialised and his cloak was dropped. His skin was spectacular in its beauty. Seemingly made from diamond, it reflected all light left in the bar, making the creature sparkle.

However, his vocal tone did not match his dazzling image. He raised his arm, and tapped another command into the wristband, before speaking into it.

"She was here. The human. The rumours were true. Inform the Captain."

Another beep later, the man lowered his wrist and reached instead for a brooch on his other arm; he vanished into thin air once more without a trace.

RESURRECTION

FOUR

Seven Years Earlier

The first explosion ruptured the hull of the ship, which lurched starboard, sending crates of supplies spilling into the corridors. The vacuum of space was now seeping into the ship.

"Warning. Hull breach on deck three. Emergency bulkheads have failed. Initiating evacuation procedures."

As Torath pulled himself back to his feet, his hair continued to change from a deep burgundy through to blackest night, and back to red again. The attack continued, without pause, and as more damage was inflicted upon his vessel, the more he began to realise he was going to need help.

"Computer, what is the status of the cryogenic units in the medical bay?"

"The cryogenic units are suffering from a sixty-five percent drop in power. They will fail in sixteen minutes, if the current rate of decline continues."

"Thank you for your words of positivity."

"Query not recognised. Please restate your question."

"Never mind."

29

As Torath continued to transfer power from other areas of the ship, the console directly in front of him beeped with a notification of an incoming message. Briefly, at least, the attack was paused.

"Torath!" a deep voice bellowed through the speakers above him.

"It's not like you to stop an attack, Lu'Thar. Usually, your victims would be speaking to you from a cloud, strumming a harp."

Sarcasm was not Torath's usual weapon of choice, but he had to make the most of the time he was being presented with. Deltarians took no prisoners. And on the rare occasions they did, death would be the preferred way out.

"I'm sure we could have a very philosophical debate on the nature of life and death, old friend, but the only reason I haven't blown you out of the sky is because I want your ship intact."

Torath hastily swiped at his control panel, issuing commands at a rate of knots. He was over three hundred years old, and yet agility was still his strongest asset. This was not the first time he had needed to defend the *Trinity*, and he had to ensure it would not be the last. The mission was too important.

"You will never take this ship, Lu'Thar. I will not allow it."

Lu'Thar laughed; a deep, belly howl to suggest the notion of him being defeated was simply impossible.

"This is not an offer, old man, it is a fact. I am going to take your vessel, and its technology. I'm simply doing you the favour of allowing you to surrender."

With a rare glance up from his console, Torath could see the Deltarian battle cruiser closing in, poised to fire the final blow. But he knew they would do no such thing. This was all a tactic to make him hand over his vessel. But he had known Lu'Thar for far too long. He thought he had him right where he wanted him. And that was all Torath needed.

"Tell me old friend, do you remember when we were students on Kizani Prime, and we used to spar in the evenings?"

A brief silence from the speakers, before a slightly less confident Lu'Thar responded.

"Now is not the time to reminisce, Torath. Hand over the Resurrection project, or we will destroy you."

Despite the threat, Torath continued his tale from their youth.

"Every night, you would defeat me, because I was using the same techniques, the same steps, and jabs, and the same footwork. You beat me every single time. I realised after all those years of being on the losing side, that I would need to change my ways. To become more unpredictable."

More silence.

"And so I began to take a leaf out of your book, Lu'Thar. You want the *Trinity* and the project, and you think I will hand it over, save it from being lost forever. Well Lu'Thar… maybe it's time you expected the unexpected."

With one punch to the console, Torath cut off the audio link.

"Computer, initiate programme Torath Delta-Six."

A loud siren echoed around the corridors, and the strip lights within the bridge and the rest of the ship began glowing red, casting a dark shadow across Torath's face.

"Torath Delta-Six has been initiated. Please prepare for emergency procedures."

In the medical bay, one by one, the cryogenics tubes began to dissolve into thin air, as if being melted into the floor. However, as the penultimate tube vanished, the *Trinity* was rocked by another impact from weapons fire, and the final tube broke free from its restraints, and fell forwards, smashing open on the floor and sending the glass everywhere.

Back on the bridge, Torath became aware of the situation, and his confidence regarding his plan was gone.

"Emergency procedures halted. Cryogenics unit four-three-nine has been compromised. Subject is no longer contained."

The instruments confirmed it. The human was no longer in stasis. Torath manually punched in the override code, and sprinted from the bridge, grabbing a weapon from the ammunition locker on his way. As he rounded the corner, he saw Molly crouched on the floor, shivering, trying to come to terms with her surroundings. As Torath approached her, she leered backwards, the sight of his appearance terrified her to her core.

"Please, do not be afraid of me," he pleaded. "We do not have much time. Do you understand me?"

Molly nodded, still unable to take in what she was seeing, eyes wide, goosebumps permanently etched into her skin.

"My name is Torath. I rescued you from Earth a long time ago. But someone is trying to stop me from saving the rest of you. And we are out of options. I need your help."

Although her brain was only partially able to process what she was being told, her vision was becoming clearer. Torath reached forward and helped her to her feet, her legs nearly collapsing several times. Once she was upright, he helped her move over to the desk of the former chief medical officer. He sat her down in the chair, and lifted up a bag from beneath it, which had been secretly hidden in a container within the desk itself.

"What… what are you?" Molly asked, not quite as out of it as she had initially been.

Torath smiled as he packed the bag with the weapon, clothing, and a few other things.

"I am a Saxon. We used to be a race of scientists, committed to the preservation of endangered species, such as yourself."

Molly found her voice.

"Endangered species? Me? You mean humans?"

Torath nodded, zipped up the bag, and swung it onto his shoulder, before helping Molly back to her feet.

"Your planet was in danger from the Decimators. I managed to reach Earth as the attack was coming to an end, and I got you up to the ship before it was too late."

Molly put her hand across his chest, stopping him in his tracks.

"What happened?" she asked, her gut swirling with the knowledge that she was too afraid to confirm. She knew what he was about to say, and suddenly the fact she was on an alien vessel, being shot at, vanished into insignificance, and the moment back in the water when she was blaming herself for the attack came rushing back to her.

"Earth was destroyed, along with its population. I'm sorry, but we have to get you to safety."

Torath found himself dragging Molly along the corridor as opposed to helping her walk, as she failed to grasp the enormity of what she had just been told. She felt like she was in a movie, or some nightmare, and that any moment, she would wake up in her bed, screaming. But it didn't happen.

As they returned to the bridge, Torath opened up a panel in the wall, which contained a chamber not too dissimilar to the cryogenic unit Molly had been in just minutes before.

"I'm sorry I don't have time to explain everything to you, or to comfort you, but take this bag. It contains everything you need to know, to help you survive, and to find me again. Good luck, human."

Before Molly had the chance to speak again, the chamber closed, and both she and the bag melted much in the same way the other cryogenic units had. Taking a deep breath, Torath turned back to the console, where the final command was awaiting execution.

"May the elders watch over us."

As Molly rematerialised inside a small scout craft, still completely unaware of what was going on, she was able to see through the window, and watched as the *Trinity* erupted in a massive blue and green fireball, debris scattering in every direction.

She slumped down in the seat, breathing rapidly, and her heel kicked the bag. But before she had a chance to look inside, the scout ship came to life, and rapidly changed direction, pinning her back into the seat.

"Welcome aboard the Aspire. Auto-pilot has been engaged. Proceeding with pre-determined flight plan."

As the *Aspire* shot out of the system, the Deltarian battle cruiser was left alone, adrift following the explosion in a sea of debris.

FIVE

The blinking of the green light above was revealing just how much drool had spread from Jaxx's mouth, as he lay on the deck-plate propped against the wall. His eyes were flickering, and a strange smile spread across his face. He was clearly dreaming, much to the entertainment of his captor.

As she checked over her rifle, she found no faults, so returned it to its holster on the wall of a tall metal locker, and removed a long narrow dagger, emerald in colour with a long hollow space in the middle of the blade itself. The handle appeared to be made of some sort of leathery material. She reached for a grinding stone, and sat back at the console, and began running the stone along the edge of the blade.

The noise clearly began to interfere with Jaxx and his dreams, as his face began to twitch and he made murmuring noises. A swift look from the pilot, and a roll of the eyes, and she turned back and continued to sharpen the dagger.

Jaxx opened his eyes in annoyance at his sleep being disturbed, before the realisation hit him that he was indeed now in reality and none of what had occurred in the bar was in fact a dream.

"Wakey wakey Sleeping Beauty."

Jaxx leapt to his feet, immediately smacking his head off the pipes embedded in the ceiling. He wiped the drool away from his face, trying to hide his slight embarrassment.

"Now listen here, you space… pirate!"

The woman chuckled.

"Space pirate? Really? What are you, like twelve?"

Jaxx looked offended.

"Actually, I'm nineteen. So… screw you."

The woman turned in her chair to look at Jaxx, admittedly surprised he claimed to only be nineteen, when he had the look and physique of someone twice that age. She squinted her eyes a little as she questioned him.

"What species are you?" she asked.

Jaxx puffed out his chest, before giving his reply.

"I, madam, am a Valkor."

The woman continued to look at Jaxx, awaiting further details, clearly completely unaware of his species, or what that meant. Jaxx did not seem impressed that she didn't know what a Valkor meant. He held out his hands in an encouraging gesture, but she shrugged her shoulders in response.

Exasperated, Jaxx laid out his species' life story.

"The Valkor were created two centuries ago, by the only humans to leave their solar system. They were designed to carry on the history of the Earth and its legacy so they would not be forgotten. When the final humans died, the Valkor learned how to reproduce and the species thrived on a planet called Koria. How do you not know the history of your own people?"

Molly put her blade down, and threw the stone back into the locker, before resting on the console and staring out of the window into the glow of the stars streaking by.

"Because I spent the last two centuries frozen like a popsicle."

Jaxx appeared confused, and sat down in the seat next to her.

"What's a popsicle?"

She chuckled again at his ignorance.

"I'm Molly," she said, looking at him through his reflection in the window.

"Jaxx. Nice to meet you Molly."

They shook hands in a way which suggested it was completely unnecessary and yet required.

"I was twenty-one when Earth was destroyed. I never left the planet. Or knew for that matter, that other humans had. We were on the way to work on the morning transport. I was a data analyst for the Defence Coalition. It was my job to analyse the output of our

39

newest weapons, and figure out ways of improving them through simulations, and mathematics. Never actually held or fired a weapon in my life. Until I was thawed out."

Jaxx chortled at that, given what he had seen in the bar.

"Yeah, you can totally tell."

Molly gave him a look of disapproval, but still with a wry smile. She continued to tell her story.

"When I came out of stasis, it was pretty much a blur. I was handed a bag of supplies, and essentially dumped out into space in this little ship by the man who rescued me. The main ship was under attack, and there seemed to be no way to save it."

"The Saxon weapon you have. It was one of them that saved you," Jaxx offered.

Molly nodded.

"Torath. He was one of the last of his kind. His ship, the *Trinity*, was an experimental design which stored thousands of examples of endangered species from all across the galaxy. He'd been rescuing people for over three hundred years."

She reached down to the left of her chair, and into the bag she had kept with her all this time. She extracted a miniature display, and tossed it towards Jaxx. As he read the information displayed on the screen, she narrated it for him.

"The Saxons were working on a way to use the DNA from the members of each species to essentially recreate that species, working backwards through their genomes, essentially, going back in time through their very makeup, and recreating their ancestors. It was called the Resurrection project."

Jaxx had never heard of anything like this before.

"What happened to it?" he asked, handing the display screen back to her.

"Torath initiated some kind of emergency procedure, evacuated the samples through teleportation, and blew up the *Trinity*."

"He blew it up?" Jaxx said, staggered at the loss of such a technology.

"Not exactly," Molly responded, with a certain reluctance in her voice. She was unsure of whether to reveal the whole truth, but something about Jaxx made her feel like she could trust him. She didn't know why, but it was a gut feeling.

"What do you mean, not exactly?"

"Torath left me instructions on how to find him again, but the file was corrupted during teleportation. If he wanted me to find him again, then he must still be alive."

"Makes sense. But how do you rescue the technology if the ship was blown up?"

Molly smiled, and pulled out the transparent chip Jaxx had been fighting Finbar for. She slipped it into the console in front of her, and a three dimensional map, and set of data appeared before them.

"This data shows records of potential sightings of the *Trinity* in several locations throughout the quadrant in the last seven years. If they are accurate, then somehow, Torath must have faked the destruction to throw the Deltarians off the scent, and vanished."

Jaxx's blood ran cold at the sound of the Deltarians.

"I've had some run-ins with them in the not so distant past."

"Is there anyone you haven't had run-ins with?"

Jaxx gave her a look to suggest he was deeply offended. After a few moments of looking at the data before him, Molly shut the program down, and put the computer module back in her pocket.

"So what's the plan?" he asked.

"We find Torath, and hopefully the *Trinity*."

Jaxx nodded in agreement. He had heard there was valuable information on the computer module, but he hadn't known what was on there. Another instinctive business deal that had gone wrong. But maybe it was going to pay off after all. He thought back to the destruction of Earth. His parents had told him about the general details, but he could never wrap his head around that scale of death and carnage.

"How long do you think it was between the initial warning, and the attack?" he asked.

Molly paused for a moment. She hadn't thought about that day for a long time. She wiped a tear from her eye, before responding.

"I got the notification on my phone at eight-forty-three. Six minutes later, I was leaping out of the back of the train carriage into the river. I reckon ten minutes from initial warning to annihilation."

Jaxx's people had always assumed it had been a long attack over several days. *Ten minutes.* That seemed impossible.

"As I lost consciousness, I saw a bright blue light under the surface, which turned out to be the *Trinity*. The rest is as I told you."

"Did you find out why the Deltarians were attacking you? You know, when you got defrosted? They clearly wanted the technology," Jaxx surmised.

Again, Molly nodded.

"Lu'Thar, their leader, believed that the technology could be adapted to not bring back individuals, but an entire planet, right down to the core. Deltaria had been a virtual wasteland, mined to death by its inhabitants for fuel, and resources. But the Resurrection project was never designed to do something on that grand a scale. Taking a couple of humans or a few members of another race was difficult enough during an apocalypse, but to save an entire world which was being mined to death by its own people,

43

was virtually impossible. Lu'Thar took this as a betrayal and decided to hunt down Torath and make him pay, and take the Trinity for himself. He figured if he could get his hands on the ship, he could be the one to perfect the technology and save Deltaria."

Molly inputted commands into the console, and the ship changed course slightly. Jaxx reached into his pocket and pulled out a water bottle, taking a swig before offering it to Molly. She politely declined.

Another beep from the console, and Molly punched in more new coordinates, the ship veering to the left, hard.

"Everything okay?" Jaxx questioned, as more parts of the console began beeping. "That doesn't sound like a very reassuring noise."

"Well, I'm not entirely certain, but I think your little stunt in the bar may have attracted some unwanted attention!"

The ship rocked from the impact of a weapons hit, Jaxx fell to the ground. As he pulled himself back to his feet, he looked through the window to see a large oval shaped vessel moving above them at a faster speed, wings to the side of the craft, glowing bright with the engines. As it moved past them, it began to drop to block their way.

"You know how to fly?" asked Molly in a rather high pitched voice.

"Please, I was flying before I was ten."

Jaxx slipped into the adjacent seat, and strapped himself in.

"Great, you fly, I'll shoot."

As Jaxx took possession of the controls, the ship lurched upwards, curving in an arc, until the ship was upside down, then twisting to starboard until it was once again the right way up, but facing the direction that it had just come from.

"Nice flying, Valkor," said Molly, as she fired the aft weapons, hitting the enemy vessel, but making no dent in their shielding.

"Yeah, I'm something of a space based superhero."

Molly smiled at Jaxx's sense of humour, which she was rapidly getting used to. Another ship of the same design appeared on the port side, and the one they had avoided behind them, was now turning to follow.

"So who are these jerks?" he asked, as he made more flight adjustments.

"Well, those saucer shaped ships belong to the Deltarian Military. A stylish new design they've come up with. Can hit speeds three times faster than their old class of vessel."

"Impressive design. Not a great turning circle though."

"Yeah well that just gives you a superhero advantage, fly boy."

Jaxx's smile was wiped from his face though, when more ships entered range of a different design. Molly offered to extend her sentence.

"And those ugly bastards are your friends, the Allurians."

There were now six ships closing in on them, and Jaxx was having to think fast.

"Anytime now Jaxx," Molly was urging some sort of action, as she continued firing their particle weapons at all ships in range.

"Yeah, yeah, let me think," Jaxx said as the vessels closed in on them.

"You don't really have the time!" Molly replied forcefully, as they took several more hits.

The next impact sent sparks shooting from the console to Molly's left, and smoke began to fill the cabin.

"Jaxx!" she shouted.

With one swift entry into the console, Jaxx initiated his most risky tactic to date. The ship lurched violently down, avoiding the incoming Deltarian vessel, which had no time to correct its course, and impacted on the initial vessel causing an immense explosion, destroying both ships in an incredible red and orange fireball, debris striking the other vessels.

"Holy shit!" shouted Molly, as she stopped firing, and held on to her seat for dear life.

Jaxx, then yanked their ship to starboard, and rotated it to a vertical angle, slipping between two oncoming Allurian warships.

"Fire then!" he shouted at Molly, who snapped out of her daze of fear and hit all the weapons she could find, sending torpedoes and particle blasts in every direction.

As the Allurian ships became disabled, and floated aimlessly in space, the remaining one Allurian vessel and the one remaining Deltarian vessel began opening fire on each other. Jaxx pulled back on the controls, and the two of them watched, bemused by what was happening.

"What are they doing?" asked Jaxx.

Molly inputted some commands into the communications array, and tapped into their feed.

"Retreat from this system you cowardous rock monsters!"

"How dare you attack a Deltarian Military vessel! You have no jurisdiction here!"

"We are Allurians! We do not need jurisdiction! We claim our prize wherever we find it!"

"This vessel is claimed by the Deltarian Military under the command of Captain Lu'Thar, General of the…"

"I do not care who commands you! You will be destroyed, and we shall claim the Saxon's prize for ourselves!"

Molly cut off the transmissions.

"I think it's safe to say they're after you," Jaxx suggested.

"Hey if I go down, fly boy, I'm taking you with me!" she responded.

"Well I'm definitely in favour of self preservation, so shall we leave?" he replied.

A single nod was all Jaxx needed, as he hit in a course, and engaged at top speed away from the battle zone. After they confirmed they were not being followed, Molly began to relax.

"So *now* where are we going?" Jaxx asked.

"Well we won't make the next reported location of the *Trinity* in this condition. We will need to go for repairs."

Jaxx looked at the coordinates, and recognised a facility less than seven light years from their position.

"Draylon Prime."

"You know this place?" Molly enquired.

Jaxx puffed out his cheeks.

"I know the station commander's wife."

Jaxx and Molly exchanged looks, before inputting the commands, and the *Aspire* altered course, and headed for the facility, with both occupants expecting a blast from Jaxx's past.

RESURRECTION

SIX

As he gazed at the report for what must have been the two-hundredth time, Lu'Thar could not help but feel the same despair that he had felt all those years ago. The image of the young girl staring back at him from his computer console was the same one that haunted his dreams at night. He could still see her twisted face as he looked on, unable to prevent her demise. His daughter had been eleven years old. An apprentice on Deltaria, with such promising potential, he envisioned her becoming one of the planets' finest artisans. He had even secured her a place at the finest university a decade before she would require it, thanks to his position. But as he closed the monitor downwards, he put those images to bed, yet again.

He still blamed himself for the accident, despite evidence to the contrary. His daughter had snuck aboard his ship which had been mining deep in the planet's core, when a collapse crippled the ship, and the crew abandoned it, launching escape pods within three minutes of the initial impact. Ruthless in their efficiency. However, as the pods left the cavern, Lu'Thar was forced to watch the terror on his daughter's face as she appeared at the window of the main bridge, looking for her father, but watching him as he left her behind.

If anything, it was this memory which spurred him on even more to save his planet. While the Deltarians were in denial about what they were doing to their planet, and had been for their entire existence, Lu'Thar felt in some way that if he saved the world, he could save his daughter. And there was something on Torath's vessel which would help him with that task.

He was interrupted by the sound of the door chiming. His office was simple, but functional. The *Challenger* was a new ship. Capable of long range travel at the highest speeds available, but provided no comfort that was not necessary. Everything on board had a function and a purpose.

"Enter."

The door rose into the frame in a vertical fashion, to reveal the form of Lu'Thar's loyal first officer, Syl'Va. The sight of this man always filled Lu'Thar's heart with a sense of achievement. He had been told by his superiors that Syl'Va lacked the potential to become an officer in the military and that no child who was scrounging for scraps of food from the slums of the mines on Deltaria could ever amount to anything of note. Syl'Va had however proved them wrong, and was now almost like a son to Lu'Thar.

"I have a report for you, Captain, from the *Sapphire*."

He handed over a tablet displaying a written account of the events of the battle involving the destruction of two Deltarian ships and two Allurian warships.

"They escaped?" he questioned, without looking up from the report.

"Yes, Sir. And the *Sapphire* took heavy damage. She is unable to make it back to our territory without assistance."

Lu'Thar had suspected his old friend had been able to give the human woman some kind of knowledge of the time she now found herself in, but she could not have learned to pilot a vessel in such a manner as was detailed in this report. She must have learned the skills from somewhere in the years since Torath sent her away. Or she had help.

"Where are they headed now?" Lu'Thar asked.

"Sensors lost them near the Draylon system."

Lu'Thar hit a panel to the left of his desk.

"Bridge?"

The comms system sparked into life.

"Bridge here, Captain."

"Alter course. Head for the Draylon system. High velocity."

"Acknowledged, Captain."

Syl'Va looked concerned.

"We are going after them personally, Sir?"

Lu'Thar placed the tablet on his desk and stood up, towering over his second in command by a clear foot. He moved alongside him, and placed a hand on his shoulder.

"We must locate the human. She has what we need. The location of the Saxon vessel. And clearly our other ships are not up to the task."

He released his first officer and moved towards the door, which again, opened upwards upon the detection of movement.

"Sir?" asked Syl'Va.

Lu'Thar paused in the doorway.

"What about the *Sapphire*?"

Lu'Thar pondered for a moment, before replying.

"They were brave soldiers. But inadequate. Purge the vessel and all those onboard."

With that statement, Lu'Thar entered the bridge, leaving his first officer stunned, but expecting the response he had been given. He opened up the tablet on his Captain's desk, and brought up the remote link to the fleet. Punching in the coordinates of the *Sapphire*, he hesitated for a moment.

53

And then he hit the command.

As the location beacon for the ship disappeared from the map, he closed the tablet, said a brief prayer for the crew of lost souls, and then walked out of the office to join his Captain on the bridge.

The immense size of the command centre of the *Challenger* had taken even Syl'Va by surprise when he had first set foot onboard. From the outside, she seemed to match the design to many Deltarian ships over the years. A single oval shape, with two swept back engines jutting out from pylons to the sides. But this was a new class of vessel. The *Challenger* was a *Celebration-Class* vessel. Designed to be the ship which saved Deltaria. The oval shape of the main body was more circular than previous models, and the two engines had been increased to three, and rather than jutting out on pylons, were attached to secondary hulls on the left, right, and central positions at the back of the main structure. This extra engine allowed the *Challenger* to hit speeds no other ship in the fleet could match.

And she could pack a punch. She held fifteen particle disruptor cannons, and seven torpedo launchers, Making her the most heavily armed ship not only in the fleet, but in the quadrant. Syl'Va was still in awe that he had been able to serve on a ship at all in the military, let alone the newest flagship. And as First Officer. As he took his station alongside Lu'Thar, the engines roared into life, and the view from the screen at the front of the bridge showed the vessel turning to starboard at speed, before launching into full flight.

The bridge itself was brightly lit. The walls were a vibrant shade of white, illuminated from behind by several lighting rigs. Six stations were dotted around the perimeter for various functions. One for engineering, one for scientific surveys, two for weapons control, allowing for a maximum attack pattern, one station for communications, and another for administration. The seventh console was located directly in front of the viewing screen and was that of the pilot. The central seat was of course occupied by the Captain, and sat higher than the two seats beside him, which were designated for the first officer, and a special envoy, such as the Chief General, should their presence be deemed necessary for a mission.

Lu'Thar felt the uneasiness from his first officer, as he took his place on the bridge.

"You are unhappy, my friend?"

Syl'Va continued to look at his personal console.

"No, Sir."

Lu'Thar turned his seat, and asked again.

"There is something troubling you, Commander. What is it?"

Syl'Va looked up, but faced directly ahead to avoid the scorning gaze of his commander in chief.

"I do not believe it was the correct course of action to purge the *Sapphire*, Sir. I believe we could have used the resources."

Lu'Thar nodded, acknowledging his viewpoint, before immediately dismissing it.

"Those crew onboard that ship failed their mission. Three ships against one tiny shuttle craft, and two meagre Allurian vessels. They are damaged beyond repair because that crew failed. They pose no useful resource to our mission, and it would take two days to rescue what remained. The decision was clear."

He spun his chair back around, considering the matter now closed.

Syl'Va, however, did not. He had been stirred and the military man inside of him was beginning to come out of his diamond-encrusted shell.

"I humbly disagree, Sir. You purge a vessel of noble Deltarians, and yet you keep your Saxon acquaintance alive, using up our resources for a distant hope, that he will cooperate and reveal the location of his vessel."

The other crew members on the bridge now looked up from their consoles, clearly nervous at the response from their Captain. Open disobedience in the Deltarian military in these times, more often than not, meant demotion, or in extreme cases, execution.

Lu'Thar turned back towards his officer, and leaned in closely.

"Torath will disclose the location of the Trinity. That is a fact. If he does not, then we will find the human and her accomplice, and we will use them to persuade him. And then we will use his technology

56

to save Deltaria. We will use every resource we have to achieve that goal. The *Sapphire* is gone. They were weak, and so was the vessel. The *Challenger* will save our planet and leave others trembling in her wake. Do I make myself clear, Commander? Or would you prefer the rank of First class Ensign in charge of scrubbing out the waste removal systems?"

One swift look up from Lu'Thar, set the rest of the bridge crew back to work, and as he glanced at a now deflated Syl'Va, he received a muffled response.

"No, Sir."

"Excellent. Then on to our destination, Lieutenant Moltar."

"Yes, Captain."

"Commander Syl'Va, you take charge of the bridge. I'm going to check on our house guest. Maybe see if I can get his hair to change colour to something which matches the décor. It's making a bit of a mess of my floor."

57

SEVEN

The console to the left of Molly exploded with such force that its entire mounting burst free and flew across the cockpit.

"I thought you said you knew the station manager's wife?!" she shouted.

"And you didn't pick up on what I meant?!" Jaxx shouted back.

"I was hoping you were joking!"

Another panel burst from the wall, showering them both with hot sparks. The vessel attacking them was the station scout ship, and was being piloted by a very angry station manager.

"He's calling us again!"

Jaxx took a deep breath and sat back down in his seat.

"Fine! Put him on!"

The image of a very angry man appeared in a hologram in front of them both, his deep red skin only enhancing the appearance of true anger.

"You vile little maggot! You are less welcome here than a Beresian with chronic diarrhoea!"

"Well come on, Cliff, that's a bit strong! I thought we were friends!"

"Don't call me Cliff, you rotten scrotum! After what you did with my wife, you're lucky I am bothering to even speak to you! Now disengage your engines, and prepare for boarding!"

"Sorry, Cliff, I can't do that. We need repairs. Well actually, now thanks to you, we need a LOT of repairs!"

More impacts and more explosions behind Molly and Jaxx, as various panels burst free from the walls. Molly rushed to extinguish a fire which had now broken out in the sleeping quarters next door. Jaxx on the other hand continued with his argument.

"I told you not to call me Cliff!"

"Well I'm hardly going to pronounce your full name, am I?!"

"I will blow you out of the sky you Valkor scum!"

Molly returned to the cockpit, and frustrated at the pounding her ship was taking, despite Jaxx's piloting skills, took over the conversation.

"Excuse me, Mr Cliff? I…"

"My name is NOT Cliff! It is Cliffordianaroxumphilopranost Grambinarona!"

Molly looked across at Jaxx, who simply shrugged his shoulders.

"Yeah I'm not saying that. So Cliff, we need to land for repairs, and you're in our way, so if you don't disengage your attack, I'm gonna open fire."

A barrage of laughter came from Cliff's face, which only served to irritate Molly further.

"Your little ship cannot match mine for firepower!"

Molly smiled at him.

"No, but yours can."

Jaxx glanced over at Molly, as she cut off communications, looking more than confused.

"What are you talking about?" he asked, as Molly began punching random looking commands into the destroyed console in front of her.

"Ever been teleported?" she asked him.

Jaxx shuddered.

"Once, and I was sick for a week. Why?"

Molly looked over and smiled at him, as she hit the final command. Jaxx's face contorted with terror as the two of them seemingly melted upwards through the hull of the *Aspire*, and flew through space, passing a red streak as they did so, which was flowing in the opposite direction. As they materialised onboard the scout ship, Jaxx continued to scream in terror, before running into the corner and vomiting violently. Cliff, meanwhile, found himself in the cockpit of the *Aspire*, now burning fiercely from his attack. He spun around looking for Jaxx and Molly, but found nothing. Items in front of him began to disappear as they too shot towards the scout ship, and as he fought through the smoke to reach the console, and looked out of the window, he saw his own ship staring back at him, with Molly now at the controls. She looked back at him with a devilish smile on her face, and opened communications once again.

"So, you give up, Cliff?"

Had his face not been a natural shade of red, Cliff's expression would have been flushed with furious rage.

"NEVER! I will blow you out of the sky with whatever weapon I have at my disposal!"

He hit what he assumed were the weapons controls, but was met instead with several minor explosions, as the hull began to crumple from the fight.

Molly shrugged her shoulders.

"Your funeral, Cliff."

She closed communications, and fired on her own ship. As the torpedoes approached, Cliff attempted to run towards the back of the ship, which of course was a futile manoeuvre, and as they impacted the ship, it exploded with immense force for a ship of such a small size, and Cliff was no more.

The explosion from the *Aspire* sent a shockwave of debris directly at the station scout ship, and the impacts along the hull battered the vessel to the point where it was immediately disabled. Explosions and bursts of smoke began to erupt all over the vessel.

Jaxx recovered enough to move back towards the front of the scout ship in time to see the last moments of the explosion.

"You blew up your own ship!" he exclaimed.

"It was that or let him blow us up," Molly replied.

She walked away to assemble her belongings that she had teleported over from the *Aspire*.

"Now what do we do?"

Molly looked at the diagnostics panel.

"Well, judging by the fact that the destruction of the *Aspire* has ruptured the fuel lines, and compromised the structural integrity, I'd say we have about five minutes to get onto Draylon Prime before we explode too."

Panic then set in and Jaxx began darting back and forth, unsure of which direction to go in.

"And how do you suppose we do that? You're crazy! And where the hell did you get a teleporter from?!"

Molly held her hand up for calm, and opened a bag to reveal the same long oblong strip she had used to carry Jaxx from the bar.

"And what exactly is that?" he asked, but did not have time to come to terms with what was happening, as once again he was encompassed by a glowing orange forcefield, which lifted him from his feet.

After sweeping her bag onto her shoulder, Molly too encompassed herself in a forcefield with a second strip, and the two of them floated in the ship. Jaxx, now consumed by fear, and restricted in movement, simply looked at Molly, waiting for some sort of explanation. She simply glanced towards him and smiled.

"Hang on to your balls," she said.

As Jaxx glanced down, he saw Cliff's red disruptor glowing brightly. As the weapon overloaded and exploded next to the bulkhead, the two of them were sucked out into space, Jaxx screaming at a level only audible to dogs. Their trajectory sent them spearing towards one of the access points to the station, whilst behind them, the scout ship followed the fate of the A*spire,* and exploded, leaving only floating debris from both ships.

As the two of them clattered into the upper level of the station, Molly looked over at Jaxx, who had now stopped screaming, but still had eyes bulging with fear. Within her forcefield, Molly fished out another small object from her pocket, and managed to attach it to her left temple. Upon activation, the device expanded and covered her entire head with a transparent mesh-like helmet. Staring on in disbelief, Jaxx shouted across to her.

"Who are you?!"

Molly disengaged her forcefield, and immediately her skin began to suffer the effects of decompression, but she had just enough time to crank open the access port, and she clambered inside, dragging Jaxx's bubble in with her, and closing the hatch behind them. As the sound of re-pressurization echoed around the chamber, she deactivated her helmet device, and Jaxx's forcefield. She had forgotten, however, that Jaxx was still at least three feet off the floor, and he clattered onto the metal flooring with a loud thud.

"What the hell was that?!" he yelled between gasping for breath.

Nursing her blistered skin, Molly didn't bother looking at him as she replied.

"You're welcome. Now we need another ship."

Still in disbelief, Jaxx continued his rant.

"Another ship? How about another brain? Or maybe another partner? You almost killed me! Twice!"

Molly opened the door into the corridor.

"Oh don't be such a big baby. You were fine, everything was under control."

"Under control? I was never in control!"

"Well then, business as usual for you, fly boy."

Molly strode ahead.

"And stop calling me fly boy!"

E I G H T

For a prison cell, the architecture within the room was immensely attractive. The holographic imagery on the furthest wall from the door, showed the rings surrounding the planet of Deltaria, and the minerals within. The picture reflected the glow from the planet's atmosphere beautifully, creating a turquoise and indigo rainbow effect which illuminated the room to remind interrogators what they were fighting for. The Deltarians were tough both on the inside and the outside.

The only known species in the galaxy with their diamond hardened skin, they were renowned bounty hunters, with extreme focus on right and wrong. Extreme to the point where they would consider no outside influences, or the particularities of a case which may have led to the outcome before them. The simple fact of the matter was, did the individual break the law, or not. If a man stole credits to feed his family who were starving, they only saw the theft. Black and white perspective.

However, despite their efficiency, and cold heartedness, recent events had skewed their usual methods, and they were being forced to take drastic action to preserve their planet. All of this meant that they were taking cases and missions based on the most value to their people, and their black and white views were now becoming more grey.

As Lu'Thar strolled past the simulated window of the room, the faint rattle of chains echoed around the otherwise empty space. The lights were on a minimum level, not needed with the rays from the planet, and yet just low enough to obscure the horror which the victim had been put through.

"I have been doing this for a very long time, my friend. You know this as well as I do. You were once a very powerful species. Those days have gone. You are the only one left. Do you truly wish to become another statistic in the history books of the universe?"

A cough and splutter came from the victim, still hanging from the ceiling. But no reply. The interrogator briefly looked towards him, and then turned back to the planet, gazing at the wonder before him, the light now twinkling within his skin.

"Simply beautiful. My home is everything to me. Everything to all Deltarians. We will do whatever is necessary to protect her. You understand that, old man?"

A brief attempt at a chuckle came from the man in chains, which caught the attention of his captor, who as he turned, cast a brief ray of light from his skin across the dangling pair of feet. Surrounding the enormous blue feet, were discarded locks of long hair. However, the hair had not been cut from its victim, it had been ripped. The hair itself, in its separate clumps on the floor, fluctuated between the most vibrant blond, to the darkest black. The dripping sound of his forest green blood hitting the metal floor now joined the symphony to accompany the rattling metal chains

"You are amused by that notion, old friend?"

"A true friend would not do what you have done to me, Lu'Thar," replied Torath, immediately followed by a laboured cough.

Lu'Thar walked towards him, and away from the picturesque view of his homeworld. He glanced around the room, admiring the craftsmanship of his people. While they were indeed almost a singular minded species in terms of ambitions and pursuits, the attention to detail for even the most distressing environments was enviable.

"Computer, raise lighting levels to maximum."

The room illuminated immediately, following a beep of acknowledgement from the speakers above the door, showcasing the room in all its true splendour, and blinding Torath as he recoiled from the higher level of illumination.

"This room is designed for interrogation," Lu'Thar began. "And yet it could easily be used as a nursery, or as an artist studio. Look at this level of detail, Torath. Murals, and paintings designed to inspire the soul, to remind those who pass through here how joyous life is, and how wonderful it can truly be. And what you would be denying yourself if you fail to cooperate."

Lu'Thar's tone shifted downwards, and he strode towards Torath with purpose, and reached forwards, grabbing a bunch of his remaining hair, and twisting it to pull the man closer to him. His crystallized face was now a mere inch away from that of the beaten and bloodied old face of Torath. He now spoke with menace, and intent, directly into the eyes of the weakened elder.

"There are people who want your vessel and are willing to provide all the resources needed to keep my planet alive for a thousand years. Resources that we cannot match. But I don't want those resources. I want the ship for myself! That technology can keep Deltaria alive *forever!* Tell me what I want to know, Torath! Where is your ship?"

Torath looked deep into his old friend's eyes and through laboured breath, gave his reply.

"I remember when you and I had similar goals, Lu'Thar. We would travel the stars seeking out new species, and helping to save those in danger of extinction. A noble quest. A dear friend to all Saxon people. To *all* people. Now look at you. Look what you have become. You're no better than the rest of your people. You were once a proud race, a valued ally to anyone. Now you've become as desperate and greedy as those that you serve."

The rage grew within Lu'Thar at the sound of those words, and with a mighty tug, Torath's hair tore free from the old man's scalp, and he screamed in intense agony, as Lu'Thar threw the fibres to the ground. As it landed, it turned to a vibrant blue, almost glowing, before fading to black. He leaned close to his old companion once more.

"You were my oldest and trusted friend. I came to you for help to save my planet, and you refused. I said we could find a way together, but you refused. I asked you for your ships' coordinates, and you refused. You have nobody to blame but yourself. What happens next is on your conscience, not mine."

And with one final swift punch across the old man's face, he was knocked unconscious, and Lu'Thar moved back towards the projection on the wall.

"Computer, restore lighting to previous levels."

The room grew dim, now once again illuminated mostly by the planet's glow. Lu'Thar's eyes began to tear up as he tried to forget how close he and Torath once were. They had been inseparable, but those days were now gone. Deltaria took priority. It was his duty, and responsibility. And he must succeed.

"Bridge, respond."

A voice echoed from the speakers above.

"Bridge here."

"Increase speed to Draylon Prime."

"Has there been a development, Sir?"

"The mission remains the same, Commander. We just have to take more extreme measures to achieve it."

"Aye, Sir. We should reach the Draylon System within two hours."

"Excellent, Syl'Va."

He turned to look once more at his unconscious prisoner.

"And, Commander?"

"Yes, Sir?"

"Send someone down to tighten our guest's restraints. They appear to have come a little loose."

NINE

"Let me ask you something."

"Go ahead. If it's an intelligent question."

"Where did you learn to do all that? And where did you get all that technology from? Teleporters are rare in this neck of the galaxy, and I've only ever seen them used by Deltarians and Allurians."

Molly flipped up the hood of her cloak as they turned into the marketplace.

"I met an arms trader about two years after I was separated from Torath, called Rilan. He was a Vargon, and he taught me how to survive. He'd had to do it for decades, and I'd come straight out of the twenty-second century in a science lab. He gave me two years of intense combat training. The rest… I had to figure out for myself."

Jaxx stopped walking.

"You didn't answer my question. Where did you get the teleporter?"

Molly stopped and turned to face him.

"I took it from Rilan's quarters on his ship. I figured, the way he was going, it would come in handy one day. And I was right."

She continued walking towards the landing pads. Jaxx followed, but he needed more information.

"What do you mean, the way he was going?"

"Let's just say he was making decisions that were putting us in precarious situations. He trained me to survive, so I employed my survival instincts. Let's leave it at that."

Jaxx grabbed hold of her arm and pulled her back.

"No. I want to know. What happened to you? You were a peaceful scientist. No amount of training from an arms dealer, would give you the skills you demonstrated back there."

Molly looked left and right, anger now on her face. She grabbed Jaxx's other arm and dragged him into the shadows, before letting go. She glanced around again, before pulling up her sleeve to reveal what looked to be some kind of symbol burned into her skin.

"You see this?" she asked.

Jaxx nodded.

"This is the mark of a slave."

Jaxx was confused.

"I don't understand."

Molly took a deep breath, before clarifying for him.

"Rilan needed a component to make a piece of equipment he had possession of, actually work. Something I figured would make us some money to help me track down the *Trinity*. But in order to get it, he had to make a trade. I was the trade."

Jaxx was horrified.

"Wait a minute. Are you telling me your friend traded you like some inanimate torpedo, just so he could make a machine work?"

"I was a young woman out of place and out of time!" Molly shouted, which attracted the attention of nearby people.

She pulled Jaxx further into the shadows.

"I was the last human in a galaxy that didn't know what to do with me, and I was naive enough to think Rilan actually cared for me and wanted to help me. So I did what I felt I had to."

"I don't care how badly you need a piece of equipment, it is not worth trading someone's life!"

"You don't understand! At the time, I was too frightened to know any different! I was in love with him, and he was all I knew!"

Jaxx looked back at her with an empty expression, and she sighed, and stormed off. He followed her closely, struggling to keep up, even with his bigger strides.

"I'm sorry, but nothing would make me trade the woman I loved into slavery!"

Molly stopped dead, and swung a punch towards Jaxx, but he ducked and charged her gut, and the two of them flew into a fruit cart, much to the dismay of the vendor. Molly attempted to hit him, but he held her arms firm.

"Please! Tell me what happened!"

"ALRIGHT!" Molly shouted.

The two of them got to their feet, brushing off the mangled fruit, before walking away from the crowd that had now gathered, and finding a quiet corner of the forecourt.

"The people who had the component we needed were Kaleys."

"Kaleys? The pirates of the galaxy? An arms dealer, dealing with pirates?"

Molly nodded. And finally Jaxx understood.

"They branded me, and they came to my room whenever they were angry, or when they were celebrating. There were forty three people on that ship. And I can remember every one of their faces as they beat me. Rilan said he would come back for me in a few days. After the first week, I still held out hope. After two weeks, the hope began to fade. I endured their ways for ten weeks before I snapped. One of them came in drunk from Dellurian Ale, and I took his knife, and slit his throat. I fought my way through that crew, using the skills Rilan had taught me, and I killed them all. One by one. And when I finally reached the bridge of their ship, I saw Rilan's

75

ship appear on the viewscreen. It was then that I decided that I would never put my trust in anyone else ever again. No matter how noble the cause, or the appearance of genuine concern or even love. I would have my own back. And I didn't need anyone else."

Jaxx collapsed to the floor in shock. He had heard of the way Kaleys dealt with women and how they even targeted children if it served their purpose. But he had never realised to the extent they conducted themselves. He was lost for words.

"I'm sorry."

Molly looked up at him, and wiped her eyes dry from her tears.

"It's fine. I'm stronger now. And I can take care of myself."

Jaxx put his hand gently on her arm.

"No. I'm truly sorry."

Molly nodded, and the two of them continued walking towards the landing pads. Eager to change the subject, Molly decided to learn more about the sarcastic rebel she had become partners with.

"So if you're only nineteen, how come you look forty?"

Jaxx was visibly wounded by this comment, but answered it nonetheless.

"Valkor reach maturity within four years. We are born as babies, like humans, but we grow to full puberty by the age of three, such was the way we were engineered by our human ancestors, and exit it by age four. It's then that our metabolism balances out, and we pretty much stay the same age for two, three hundred years, and then we hit our old age, and the process activates again. We age sixty years within four. Then we die."

"Wow. That's messed up. So you're a kid for a couple years, spend a year letting your balls drop, live looking forty for two centuries, then hit old age and rot in the space of four years."

"We don't rot, thank you very much. We, age like a fine wine. Only much, much quicker."

"So in all your life, have you ever actually seen them?"

"Seen who?"

"The Decimators."

Jaxx stopped cold in his tracks, and Molly stopped as soon as she noticed.

"Are you okay?" she asked.

"Please don't say that name, Molly."

Molly's expression turned to one of concern, as soon as she saw the look of grief on Jaxx's face.

"I'm sorry, I didn't mean to upset you."

"No, it's… it's fine. But, that name brings back a lot of painful memories for my people."

"Yeah, mine too, remember."

Jaxx shook his head as they continued walking.

"No, you don't understand. They destroyed a planet in our system, and left without thinking about the collateral damage they would cause. It's kind of their modus operandi. They do what they want and screw the consequences. Our planet was an ocean paradise. But when they wiped out Aegon IV, the shift in gravity caused our world to move nearer to our sun. The oceans dried up, and most of my people died of thirst. Or burned to death. I was one of the lucky ones. I was born after all this happened. My parents were colonists themselves. They settled us on a nice little planet far away. But they told me the stories as a child. They told me how the… Decimators, destroyed our ancestors on Earth, and countless other worlds. And then, just vanished."

Molly held up her hand apologetically.

"What do you mean they vanished?"

"When the Decimators deemed their mission a success, and that they had eliminated all known species they deemed 'lesser' they retreated back to their own space on the edge of the galaxy, never to be heard from again."

"How long ago was that?"

"One hundred and seventy five years ago."

"And nobody has ever ventured into Decimator territory?"

Jaxx shook his head.

"Nobody has ever come back, anyway."

Molly pondered this for a few minutes, before spotting an unguarded ship on the third landing pad. She alerted Jaxx to her find, and the two of them made a move in that direction. Suddenly, a thought occurred to her.

"So if the Decimators retreated to their space believing their mission was done, what would they do if they knew they had failed, and there was still a human, or a Saxon running around freely."

Jaxx looked her deep in the eyes.

"Let's hope we never find out."

Molly nodded in agreement. That kind of power was not welcome.

Jaxx then had a thought, and despite them moving on from the previous subject, couldn't help but ask the question.

"So what happened to that Rilan guy?"

Molly smirked, and checked that her rifle was still in its holster, never breaking her gaze.

"I killed him."

TEN

"Initial scans, Commander?"

"Current station population is six-thousand-fifty-two. It consists of seventeen different species."

Lu'Thar gazed at his first officer, urging him into more specific details.

"We are too far away at this moment in time to detect exactly which species there are. However, there is a debris field surrounding the station which indicates a recent fire fight."

Lu'Thar stood from his chair and moved towards the front of the bridge, observing Draylon Prime, stood legs shoulder width apart, hands clasped behind his back.

"What kind of debris is that?" he asked.

The tactical officer was the first to respond, which given her lower rank, irked Syl'Va, who in Deltarian tradition is already meant to know everything the Captain is going to ask of him. But his mind was not on the task. He was still thinking of the two-thousand fellow Deltarians whom he had been forced to vaporise.

"The larger pieces of debris appear to be from the station's standard scout ship, Sir."

Lu'Thar glanced over his shoulder.

"And the smaller pieces?"

The tactical officer patched a few commands into her console, before returning with the answer.

"The smaller fragments are from… a Saxon transport vessel."

Most of the bridge crew looked up at their Captain, on hearing that a vessel from a species long dead was recently in the system. Lu'Thar, however, did not alter his expression, or his stance. After all, he had a Saxon elder in chains in the brig. The crew were being kept on a need to know basis regarding that matter. The only crew who were aware were the security officers in charge of the brig, Lu'Thar, and Syl'Va.

"Bring us in, and make it appear we wish to dock with the station, Ensign."

"Yes Captain."

The helmsman altered the trajectory of the *Challenger*, and began an approach towards one of the outer docking ports, for the larger vessels. But Syl'Va was troubled by the phrasing of his Captain's words.

"*Appear* that we wish to dock, Sir?" he asked, with a definite fear in his voice for what may be about to come next.

"We have no intention of docking at this pirate port, Syl'Va. I want to know if the human is on board, take them, and then purge the area."

There it was again. Purge. That word was rapidly becoming a stomach-churning presence every time Syl'Va heard it. He wished his commander would simply say what he meant. *Murder.*

"Is that necessary, Sir? The people on the station are mostly innocent bystanders. And the trade which comes through here may prove valuable to us in the future."

Lu'Thar smiled to himself, at the sound of his first officer attempting to justify not removing this barge of metal from the skies. The truth was that some useful trade did come through the Draylon system, but not enough to justify allowing the criminals who frequented the facility to go unpunished. The Deltarian way may have been forced to adapt, but they were still, in essence, the police of the galaxy.

"Are we close enough for a detailed scan yet, Ensign?"

"Yes Captain, full details coming in now."

"Here is an educational lesson for you, Commander Syl'Va. Ensign, how many known criminals or repeat offenders are currently on that station?"

"One-hundred-sixty-four."

The list with mugshot photographs began streaming down over the window at the front of the bridge in holographic form.

"And how many of those criminals have committed murder in some form or another?"

More taps into the console.

"Ninety-seven."

"Ninety-seven. Nearly a hundred killers on that station, Syl'Va. That's a hundred killers, negotiating with perhaps a hundred terrorists, who buy their goods and materials from perhaps another hundred arms dealers, and so the chain goes on. The number of lives dispatched will far be outweighed by the number of lives saved."

Syl'Va could not believe what he was hearing. His Captain was justifying genocide of over six thousand people, rather than arrest ninety-seven. The old ways of black and white justice no longer applied, but it appeared that Lu'Thar was attempting to use both methods. The grey areas were ideal when they suited his purpose, but then the right or wrong equation came roaring back to justify actions such as this. Syl'Va was not sure how much longer he could go on following the orders of someone he used to idolise, gradually slipping into the suit of a madman.

"Ensign, is the human on board?"

"I'm unable to tell, Captain. There are sixty-three individuals who are masking their biosignature somehow. I can tell you that twenty of those are in the landing bays, and two are using what appears to be Saxon technology. But I am unable to get a precise fix on their location."

Lu'Thar turned on his heels, marched back to his chair, and sat down with force, punching several commands into his panel on the right hand side of the chair. He opened communications with the station.

"Draylon Prime, this is the Deltarian vessel *Challenger*. Please respond."

A few seconds went by, before a face appeared on the screen where the criminal activity reports had been moments before.

"This is Draylon Prime acknowledging your signal *Challenger*. How may we be of assistance?"

Lu'Thar did something that Syl'Va had never seen him do before. He turned on the charm.

"Well, if it isn't too much trouble, we would like to dock at your wonderful facility for some respite. We've been on a long journey, and we will be heading home shortly. We may be in need of minor repairs, a few of the systems on this new vessel are acting up. We'd be very grateful if you could lend some of your legendary hospitality to our crew."

That same crew appeared taken aback by this new Captain that had suddenly appeared before them. Syl'Va however, knew that this was going to turn sour, and very soon.

"Well we do try our best to meet the needs of all of our clients, Captain, but it's very kind of you to say so. Please head for docking port seven, and we will have repair crews standing by for you. Have a wonderful day."

The communication ended, and immediately Lu'Thar's face regained its stern, military focus. He punched commands into his chair console again, before signalling security.

"Bridge to Security?"

"Security here, Sir."

"Prepare a twelve person boarding party. Your mission is to transport over to the station, find the human, and return to the ship before we reach the docking ports."

"Understood, Captain."

Lu'Thar glanced over at his first officer.

"Oh, and Commander Syl'Va will be leading the team personally."

"Understood, Sir. Security out."

Syl'Va felt a knot in his stomach, and looked down at the floor. He was about to be tested, and he didn't know what the outcome would be.

"You will find the human, Commander. Our mission is the same for all of us, remember that. You either come back with the human, or don't bother coming back at all."

"Sir?"

"You heard me."

Syl'Va's bluff had been called. The Captain no longer had faith in his second in command. The questioning in front of the crew, the lack of response time in the earlier questions. He felt the eyes of the tactical officer in his back. Lieutenant Fay'Lar was not to be trifled with. She had coveted the first officer role ever since she had been assigned to the *Challenqer*, but Lu'Thar had chosen loyalty over efficiency. But that would not happen again. Syl'Va had a terrible feeling that this may be his last mission of any kind.

His thought process was interrupted by the Captain's booming voice.

"How long before we reach the docking port, Ensign?"

"Sixteen minutes, Sir."

Lu'Thar turned back to Syl'Va.

"You have fifteen minutes to get over there, get the human and get back. Because in sixteen minutes, I'm blowing Draylon Prime apart."

RESURRECTION

ELEVEN

"So… are we doing this, or what?"

Jaxx was getting rather impatient at staring at a ship. He wasn't a fan of Draylon Prime, and was constantly on the lookout for someone he may have screwed over in recent memory that would perhaps like the thought of a Valkor skin hanging on their wall. But Molly was staring intently at the maintenance crews surrounding the vessel.

"They're finishing up an install on the new engine manifold. You wanna try and steal a ship that doesn't fly? You'll end up a sitting duck for security. And judging from the look of this shit hole, they're the kind who shoot first, shoot some more, and then when everybody is dead, try and ask a question or two."

She did have a point. Jaxx instinctively moved his left hand to a small scar on his neck. A memento from one of his previous visits here. His thought process was interrupted by a beeping in his pocket.

"Damn. The bio-mask is glitching. How's yours?"

Molly checked out the small blue device in her pocket.

"Mine is working fine. Maybe you knocked it on the bulkhead when you tripped over those apples."

88

A cheeky smile spread across her face. Jaxx wasn't impressed.

"Hey, you were the one who distracted me with thoughts of Decimators hunting us down. It's not my fault a fruit stall magically appeared in front of me. Besides they weren't apples, they were Brain Burners."

Confusion replaced the smile on Molly's face.

"Brain Burners?"

"Picture an apple infused with spice to the point where you need to drink ten litres of water just to quell the fire on your tongue."

"Why would you wanna eat that?"

"Not all species have such a weakness for heat in their food, little miss princess."

Molly turned her attention back to the ship, where finally, the crews were closing up the intakes.

"Okay, let's go."

"How are we gonna get past the security guards? We look a little conspicuous don't you think? Not everyone can stroll through a checkpoint wearing a Saxon cloak."

But Molly had a plan. This wasn't the first grand theft auto she had needed to pull since coming out of deep freeze. She signalled for Jaxx to hang back against a maintenance hatch. As two workmen cleared the checkpoint and headed for the food court, she casually checked out the surrounding area. Nobody that would interfere. Perfect. She walked forwards, as if to move between them, and as they drew level, a swift elbow to the gut to the person on the left, and a scorpion kick to the face for the second, knocked both to the ground. Followed with a swift punch across the jaw for both, before she dragged them back towards Jaxx. As suspected, everyone was too busy engaging in their own business to get involved in a distraction that may get them found out.

"That was a little bold wasn't it?" he asked when she dumped the men at his feet.

"What? You were right, so I came up with a solution."

Gesturing towards the maintenance hatch, Jaxx opened it up, and he, Molly, and their two victims disappeared into the wall, emerging moments later without the unconscious workers, but with the maintenance outfits they had previously occupied, draped over their own clothes.

"That was such a cliched trick," Jaxx muttered as he giggled to himself.

"Sometimes, the classics are the best."

That was hard to argue with, as it had indeed helped them to blend in. But their troubles were far from over. As Jaxx glanced up, he noticed a detail about the security guarding the vessels that he hadn't picked up on before. He grabbed Molly's arm, and pulled her to the side.

"What's the matter?" she asked.

Jaxx nodded towards the guards. They were Allurians.

"If we get too close to them without having a plan, we'll be worse than dead."

Molly thought about that for a moment, as something had been troubling her since she found Jaxx in the bar.

"You didn't really... romance Finbar's wife did you?"

"That's probably best left out of your imagination."

The visible goosebumps on Molly's skin, agreed with that notion. But she was still without a crucial element to their strategy. She did have one idea, but it would expose them to anyone with a scanning device.

"I could modify the bio-mask devices to convert them to a minor explosive that would knock out an Allurian in close proximity, if needed of course. But there are two negatives to that idea."

"Let's hear them."

"One, engineering isn't my speciality, so there's no guarantee it would actually work."

Jaxx waited impatiently.

"And the second?"

"Our bio-signs would be detectable to anyone looking for us. We'd be a huge target for someone looking to claim the last human or an endangered Valkor."

Given their near miss with the Deltarians and the Allurians that essentially cost them their last ship, the risks were incredibly high. But they needed that ship. It was more dangerous to stay put than keep on the move.

"Well, you get the devices modified, and I'll get the red and white paint for our backs."

Molly smiled, and began the changes. She had only known Jaxx a week, but she admired how he didn't tend to shy away from the dangerous scenarios. He screamed a lot, definitely, but he always came through. She couldn't afford to tell him yet though, how that encounter in the bar was far from a chance meeting. He was too useful to her at this point.

With the modifications complete, Molly took a deep sigh, and handed Jaxx's back to him.

"That's it, we're exposed."

Jaxx held out a fist, and the two bumped hands.

"Then let's get to it."

As they approached the guards, they seemed to be too distracted to pay any attention to the pair anyway. Their gaze was captured by something else. Tempted to look away from his target, Jaxx kept his focus, and they walked through the checkpoint unopposed. As they entered the landing pad though, it was still troubling him. Molly was attempting to gain the access codes to the ship, when he broached the subject.

"Didn't that seem a little too straight forward to you?"

Molly's attention didn't wane, but she agreed.

"Yes, far too easy. Clearly something is up, but we don't have the time or the ability to stick around and find out if we wanna get out of here, so I'm not even looking."

Jaxx however, was far too curious to not have a quick glance. And that glance amped up the fear by a thousand percent. As he looked over at the checkpoint, he saw the Allurian guards running towards a scuffle that had broken out near the vent that he and Molly had stashed the workmen in. But it wasn't the work men that had been discovered. It was a group of Deltarians. Jaxx counted thirteen, but only seven were engaged in the brawl. The other six were scanning the area with devices, and as Jaxx moved his gaze from the fight to them, their scanners must have detected his presence, because they looked right at him.

"Erm… how much longer are you gonna be?" he asked with a slight tremble in his voice.

"A couple of minutes, why?"

"Oh no reason. There's just a team of Deltarians running towards us with weapons aimed. So you know, no pressure."

Molly's head snapped up, and she too saw the group running towards them, storming the security checkpoint. The Allurians were strong, broad creatures, but no match for the Deltarian Military. The lead officer and two of his crew began firing blasts from their disruptors, the initial shot just missing Jaxx's shoulder, and hitting the hull of the ship, sending orange sparks over Molly.

"Shit. I guess this isn't going to go quite as smoothly as I'd hoped."

Molly's words came as something of an understatement and Jaxx dove for cover. Molly however, reached behind her, grabbed hold of either side of the maintenance uniform, and pulled it, tearing down the spine, and exposing her usual cloak and weaponry. Jaxx looked on in awe, as she slid a long Saxon blade from one holster, and a disruptor rifle from the other, and charged at the oncoming soldiers.

Jaxx couldn't believe what he was seeing. Who was this woman? She'd been out of the ice for seven years, had a bit of training and then gone vigilante for the last five or so, and now she was acting like some sort of action hero from a movie. But he'd grown fond of her, and knew she wouldn't last alone. He pulled the mini explosives from his pocket that used to be their bio-masks, and tossed them into the path of some Allurian reinforcements, who stepped on the devices and were immediately blown apart. Jaxx felt a sharp shift in the contents of his stomach at such a sight, but

94

knew he needed to focus. He grabbed his own disruptor from his holster, took a deep breath and lunged from behind the console he'd been sheltering at. Molly was firing shots in every direction, hitting a few Deltarians, but not enough to knock them back. Having a skin encrusted with one of the hardest substances in the galaxy certainly had its benefits.

Jaxx however, knew they had a soft spot. He just had to get a shot away. Molly leapt up onto one of the pallets stationed near the checkpoint, and with a quick jump, and twirl through the air, she landed her blade directly in between one of the Deltarian officer's shoulder blades. He screamed in agony, as she rolled down his back, and launched a tirade of weapons fire at the next nearest attacker.

The other brawl between the Deltarians and the Allurian guards had now come to an end, and the full force of the boarding party sent down by the *Challenger* was now closing in on them. All except Syl'Va. He stood back and watched on. The movements of this human woman seemed to be off. It was almost as if she had been training for combat her entire life. But he knew this to not be the case. The way she dodged blows, and swung her blade reminded him of his own military training. But surely that was impossible.

His attention was grabbed by his communicator signalling an incoming transmission.

"Syl'Va, progress report."

He despaired at the booming voice of his Captain. The more he watched this woman, the more he felt that there was something else going on here. Even her Valkor accomplice seemed taken aback at her fighting skills. She had managed to take down five of his soldiers at this point. He felt like something was being hidden from him. And he didn't like it.

"We have located the human. A female, and she has a Valkor helping her."

"A Valkor? Interesting choice, human. You have six minutes left, Commander. Capture the human, kill the Valkor, and return to the ship."

The communication ended abruptly. Syl'Va drew his weapon, but was hesitant to move forward. This woman was more than a human. There were far too many questions here, and Syl'Va no longer felt that he was in his Captain's confidence. In fact, he had a sneaking suspicion that if he did return to the ship, he may not return to his position as first officer, and end up hanging in chains next to the Saxon prisoner. He decided to hang back, but kept a watch on the time. Five minutes left before his Captain committed yet another atrocity. No more. There had been enough death.

Syl'Va looked around as Molly took down her seventh soldier, and Jaxx his first. He spotted an alarm node located on a wall just above the security checkpoint. He aimed his disruptor and fired at the node, causing it to blow apart, showering those beneath it with glass and green sparks. Immediately the evacuation alarm sounded,

96

and a frantic scramble for the airlocks and landing pads began. All around him, panic was setting in.

The Deltarian soldiers who remained, were also distracted by the alarm, as was Molly. A little too distracted, as it happened. One of the soldiers reacted quickest and fired his disruptor at Molly. As Jaxx watched on, she flew backwards and landed in a pile of rubble. He froze on the spot as the soldier charged towards him, weapon raised. Jaxx looked down at Molly, who was no longer moving, but he couldn't move himself. Waiting for the inevitable, he was surprised when the Deltarian screamed in pain, a blade penetrating his chest between the diamond layers. As the blade was retracted, the body crumpled to the floor, revealing Syl'Va standing in his place. Jaxx raised his weapon, but Syl'Va held up his hands, and pleaded for a ceasefire.

"No, please, wait. I am not your enemy, but we must get you both out of here as soon as possible."

Molly murmured in the corner, much to the relief of Jaxx, but her wound was now clearly visible, and she was losing blood. A lot of blood. The left side of her stomach had been hit, and the fabric was turning a dark crimson.

"Why should I trust you?" shouted Jaxx.

Syl'Va couldn't answer that but he did reiterate the need to leave and quickly.

97

"You can't, I understand. But if you don't get out of here, my Captain is going to blow up this station and everyone on it! You need to get on that ship and get out of here!"

The remaining four soldiers that had now witnessed their Commander betraying his oath charged towards him, blades raised, and disruptors firing. Syl'Va took two hits to the shoulders, but remained on his feet.

"GO!" he shouted.

Jaxx turned and ran towards Molly, picking her up, and carrying her as fast as he could to the ship. As she opened her eyes, she looked up at Jaxx, and smiled.

"I told you it would be a walk in the park," she said.

"Oh yeah, a real piece of cake."

Jaxx briefly looked back as he reached the ship, to see Syl'Va was quite a formidable fighter. He had dispatched three of his own men in quick style, and was now alternating between the other two. Why was he helping them? Something was not adding up here. And Jaxx didn't like unsolved mysteries. So he made his decision.

Entering the ship, he placed Molly down on the floor carefully, and she handed him the chip containing the startup routine she had downloaded from the console. He slid it into the command panel, and the ship began to come to life. Initiating what the computer told him was the auto launch sequence, he turned back towards the door, and picked up Molly's sword, before charging back into the foray.

Syl'Va was tiring. His years of training had served him well, but one man against five was still a pretty unwinnable scenario. As he delivered the death blow to one of his former Lieutenants, he himself received a disruptor blast to the stomach, and was knocked onto his back. The soldier advanced towards him, as he struggled to get back to his feet, and addressed his former commanding officer, with a look of disgust on his face.

"You are a traitor! How can you slay your own kind to protect these pathetic creatures? The Captain was right to doubt you!"

Syl'Va admitted that he had taken a rather drastic turn away from the path laid out for him, but he needed to uncover the truth. And he couldn't do that on board the *Challenger*.

"The Captain isn't telling us what's really going on here. He's lying to us, and he's killing innocent people along the way. You have to listen!"

The soldier spat on the ground.

"I will not listen to the lies of a traitor. But I will kill you!"

He fired a blast from his disruptor, and Syl'Va ducked down at the last minute. As he glanced back up, he saw a blade twirling through the air, almost in slow motion. As he followed its path with his eyes, he watched it bury itself in the chest of his former colleague, and with an exasperated breath, he fell to his knees, before collapsing fully to the ground.

Syl'Va spun around to see Jaxx running towards him. He held out a hand and Syl'Va took it, nodding in thanks to Jaxx, who moved over to the dead Deltarian and retrieved the blade from his chest.

"Shall we go then?" asked Jaxx.

Syl'Va, simply nodded again, and the two ran onto the ship, where Molly had pulled herself into the pilot's chair, applying pressure with one hand to her wound, and punching commands into the console with the other.

"You know, to activate an auto-launch, you actually need to activate the auto-pilot itself," she said through laboured breath.

Jaxx felt a little embarrassed, but grateful he had Molly to help him out of yet another tricky situation. As the loading doors were sealed, the ship raised from the pad, but as the auto-pilot engaged, the ship rocked from a hit to the hull from below. An audio message echoed around the bridge.

"Auto-pilot has been damaged. Repairs were not fully complete at launch. Manual override required."

Molly's eyes rolled back in her head, and she fell out of the chair onto the floor.

"Molly!"

Jaxx ran to her side, but felt a hand on his shoulder.

"I'll take care of her, you get us out of here."

Syl'Va's tones were reassuring for a Deltarian, and Jaxx accepted his help, launching himself into the seat, and taking over the controls. The remaining security that had not been dispatched were now firing particle blasts as the departing ships to prevent them from leaving. And the space doors were still closed.

"The launch doors won't open!" he shouted.

Syl'Va looked down at his wrist.

"I don't think you'll have to worry about that," he replied.

"Why is that?" asked Jaxx.

"Because we are out of time."

As Syl'Va's timer ran down to zero, he closed his eyes, and the entire station began to rock with the impact of weapons fire. Explosions were forming in a chain reaction ahead of them, and the firing from the surface ceased as flames engulfed the landing pads. The controls starting blinking and alarms were beeping in a frenzied state.

"What the hell is that?!" Jaxx exclaimed.

"My Captain decided to purge the station before he even got here. He ran out of patience."

As the structure around them began to blow apart, Jaxx spotted an opening ahead of him. A small gap had appeared between the two massive doors as they crumpled from the stress of the attack. It wasn't big enough for the ship, but it was his only chance. He scoured the console for the weapons controls but found nothing. The audio warning. Perhaps the ship had voice control. He had no time to think it through.

"Computer, where are the weapons controls?" he asked.

Immediately he received a response.

"Weapons controls are located to the aft of the bridge. Would you like me to reroute them to the propulsion console?"

"No! Can you fire them if I give you a target?"

"Affirmative. I am capable of controlling the entire ship if necessary."

Jaxx was not appreciative of the calm manner in which the ship was responding to the situation. And he could swear there was a note of sarcasm in there too.

"Then target the launch doors with every weapon we have!"

"Target has been acquired."

Jaxx's eyeballs were now at full bulging capacity.

"THEN FIRE!!!"

A barrage of blue energy beams and torpedoes erupted from the front of the ship at higher speed than the ship itself was travelling, and the resulting impacts blew the doors apart, and Jaxx saw open space. He punched the ship to the fastest speed he dared and the vessel blew through the flames and debris into the vastness of space, clear of the station's perimeter.

"Yeah!" he shouted as he brought the ship around.

He watched as the entire Draylon Prime structure blew apart. They had barely escaped with their lives, but he was quickly reminded by Syl'Va that it was time to leave.

"Don't celebrate, we aren't out of the woods by any means."

"What do you mean?" asked Jaxx.

"What do you think destroyed the station?" Syl'Va responded.

Almost on cue, a shadow formed over Jaxx's console, and as he looked up in front of him, the vastness of the *Challenger* came into view.

"Time to go?" he asked sheepishly.

"Yeah! Time to go! Right now!" Syl'Va blasted, having finally lost his calm.

Jaxx swerved the ship to port and increased speed, taking him below the belly of the *Challenger,* an old trick he had picked up to evade weapons locks. It seemed to take forever to pass underneath this huge vessel, and just as they moved from beneath its shadow, and Jaxx went to hit top speed, they came to a shuddering halt.

"What the hell is that?" Jaxx exclaimed, unaware of what had them snared.

Syl'Va moved to one of the other consoles.

"The *Challenger* has us in an energy tether."

"A what?"

"Let's just say we've been hooked like a fish."

As Jaxx's shoulders deflated with defeat, a communication appeared on screen. Lu'Thar appeared to be even less impressed than usual.

"Commander Syl'Va. Are you leaving us?"

Syl'Va felt extreme nausea in the pit of his stomach.

"I'm sorry Captain, I can't let you take these people. Something isn't right here."

Lu'Thar burst into rage, and smashed his own chair console apart before standing and charging towards his own view screen.

"You are a traitor! You sounded the alarms to evacuate the criminals from that station! You found and protected the human! You were like my own child!"

"I'm sorry Captain, but I cannot let you justify saving Deltaria with repeated acts of murder and genocide!"

"And I will not simply let you escape, Commander. I will tear your body apart myself. I will rip those gems from your skin one by one and use them to adorn my office. And then I will extract the information I want from the human."

Syl'Va looked around the consoles frantically, before stumbling upon an idea at the back of his head. He remembered that part of the *Challenger*'s earlier notes when she was being built, were that the shielding was weakened during use of the tether and during scout ship launches. He was hoping that this had not been rectified just yet.

"No Sir, I don't believe you will."

Syl'Va cut the communication and Lu'Thar's confused face was wiped from the screen.

"What are you doing?" asked Jaxx.

"Throwing the fish back in the water."

Syl'Va targeted the weapons on the source of the tether, and fired. The beams and torpedoes impacted in a circular motion around the source itself, and sliced a section out of the *Challenger*'s hull. The tether beam terminated, and their ship was freed. The effect seemed to inflict more damage than even Syl'Va had thought. Secondary explosions emanated from the surrounding sections, and the lights within the engines of the *Challenger* flickered, before going out all together.

"What did you do?!" Jaxx exclaimed, now consumed with relief and excitement.

"I'm not entirely sure, but I don't think we want to hang around and find out, am I right?"

"Definitely!"

And as the *Challenger* lumbered to starboard, drifting without its engines, their new getaway ship hit top speed, and vanished in a flash of light.

RESURRECTION

107

TWELVE

Wherever this place was, it was incredibly dark. No natural light was visible, and just the barest of hints at colours. She could see a distant swathe of burnt orange, and a slight glow of red in the distance. As she squinted her eyes, she could make out what appeared to be floating rocks, but… that *smell*.

The smell was unmistakable.

The fumes of toxic flesh filled her nose, and while she tried to stop the deep breaths she was taking, she found she had no control over her body at all. Her skin felt icy cold, but her insides were contracting with immense pain. It felt like a thousand icy blades penetrating her abdomen and her throat. She tried to scream, but no sound passed her lips.

Suddenly, there was an eruption of brightness, as the full imagery came into view, and then she knew where she was. The fragments of the planet were vastly spread across the space before her, and as her lifeless body meandered through the debris, the faces of the remainder of the human race, all turned to look at her, their eyes wide open. In unison, they all began to raise their arms, until every one of the billions floating before her had their fingers pointed directly at her. Women, children, men, all pointing at her with their dead hands... and the eyes.

Their vacant eyes bore into her own, and she felt their presence inside her mind. The dull drone began, as each of the victims of Earth began to utter the same three words.

"It… was… you…"

As her eyes snapped open, Molly shot bolt upright in the medical bed, her hands gripping the sides tightly. Her breathing was incredibly rapid, and as she began to compose her vision and focus, and become familiar with her surroundings, she recognised a welcome face.

"You really had me going for a minute there."

Molly managed a smile, and tried to subdue the imagery from her nightmare that was still swimming around in her head. She released her grip from the bed, and lay herself back down, her eyes now adjusting to the high levels of bright light in the room.

"I've been in worse situations," she replied.

Jaxx grinned an uncertain smile. Behind him, a console began beeping, and Molly squinted enough to just see the words 'Match Found.'

"What's that?" she asked, leaning her head further to the left.

"Oh nothing, just trying to get used to the database on this luxury liner you hijacked."

Jaxx reached behind him, and switched off the monitor, before getting up and walking over to Molly's bedside.

"So, be honest, how do you feel? I thought you were gone there."

Molly instinctively reached down and ran her hand across her abdomen. There seemed to be no trace of a wound, and yet she could feel a tender spot.

"Yeah. That's actually the first time I have come that close to death in a very long time. I'm not gonna lie, it was a little scary."

Jaxx nodded. He had been in some form of danger basically every other week for his entire life. Danger was just part of the job. But for Molly, it almost seemed like an addiction. Especially judging from what he had discovered on the computer.

"So where is our new friend?" she asked, which took Jaxx by surprise a little.

"You remember that?" he asked.

"I was pretty out of it, but I do remember a random Deltarian, and having to remind you how to use a navigational system."

Jaxx shrugged the embarrassment off quickly, and changed the subject.

"Yeah, seems we bagged a defector of sorts. Lu'Thar's right hand man for the last four years apparently. Seems your old friend Torath is definitely not in his good books anymore, as you suggested."

"Lu'Thar is something else."

"What do you know about him?"

Molly stood up and moved towards the food dispenser.

"Water. Cold."

A metallic whooshing sound echoed around the unit's chamber, before a glass dropped down and began filling with water. Molly took the glass, downed the entire thing, and replaced the glass, where it was swept to the side, and the machine powered down.

"Thirsty?" asked Jaxx.

"I've been asleep with a hole in me for... how long?"

"Eighteen hours."

"Eighteen hours? No wonder I'm hungry."

Jaxx chuckled, but made his point.

"Stop changing the subject. You said he turned on Torath because he wouldn't help him save his planet."

Molly nodded.

"That's the overall gist of it, yeah. But from Torath's personal logs, there seemed like there was more to it."

"How so?"

The door to the medical bay opened, and Syl'Va walked in.

"Lu'Thar isn't interested in saving Deltaria. He's interested in saving his soul."

The two of them looked at Syl'Va, who held up a hand in apology for butting into their conversation.

"Sorry, didn't mean to butt in."

Molly held up her own hands.

"Don't worry about it, you were saying?"

Syl'Va leaned on a control panel.

"Lu'Thar is convinced that your Saxon friend has hidden his vessel, and that he has perfected the regeneration chamber to reconstitute matter, and a DNA sample, into the original form of life. For example, it you had a sample of human DNA, and the same amount of mass that the human would be comprised of, then you could recreate that exact human."

Jaxx stopped him there.

"Mass from what? Like another body, or just random material?"

"Lu'Thar believes that the device reorganises any matter and uses the DNA as the blueprint, and turns whatever that matter used to be, into the same material that the DNA came from. You could put seventy-five kilos of brain burners into it, with some human DNA, and the machine would change the fruit into a human. As long as the mass was roughly correct, the process would work."

"But the chamber is contained inside of a vessel. How could you get a planet's volume of any material into something that small?"

Syl'Va held his hands up in defeat.

"I don't know, Jaxx. That's why I think he has an ulterior motive."

Molly thought hard for a moment.

"So you think he wants to use the machine for something else? For, someone else maybe?"

Syl'Va nodded.

"He is a dangerous man, and an increasingly violent man. But he is not a stupid man. He wants *something*. And if he can save the planet in the process then he will. But that isn't his goal."

Molly was confused by this notion. All of the data she had read from what Torath had left her suggested that the technology was going to pull genetic structures from genomes and recreate other members of the same species, not clone existing ones. The situation was becoming more cloudy as the time went on. She caught a beeping noise come from Jaxx's console. Jaxx waved away the alert on the panel behind him which had reappeared once again. Molly was curious about what he was up to, but she was more interested in their new ally.

"Why did you leave his ship? Surely you didn't just switch to the power of good during the fight?"

Syl'Va's mood became reflective as he pondered just how far he had come from trusting his Captain in such a short space of time.

"He lost who he was. When he came and found me in the mines as a boy, he saw something in me nobody else did. He told me I was strong and that I could be a military leader one day. I laughed at him. But he took me under his wing. He taught me the values of our people, and our history. How we were essentially the line of justice stretching across the galaxy. Then he changed. One day he was like a father to me, and the next he was completely consumed by his task. He began acting erratically, pushing the construction crews of the *Challenger* to increase productivity levels, making them work twenty-four hour days. He didn't seem to be taking orders from above, like he was on his own. Then I learned about your friend, Torath. He'd captured him hiding out on a moon in the Gantaran Nebula."

Molly's spine ran cold at the mention of the nebula. That was where she and Rilan had attempted to barter the technology from the Kaleys. Clearly Torath had attempted to barter with them too if he had been captured there.

Jaxx was pondering new information of his own. He'd been reading the report he had accessed on the console behind him, while Molly had been distracted. But he didn't want to let on what he knew, and so he abruptly paused the conversation.

"Well, we can't do much from here. Let's move this to the bridge. I need to brush up on the navigational computer, as Molly so kindly pointed out."

Both Molly and Syl'Va were slightly put off by the change in pace, but agreed and the two of them walked through the door. As Jaxx followed them out, the console came back to life, and as the door closed, the lights dimmed. The room was dark, all but for the light of the glowing console, displaying Molly's picture, and the words 'Wanted for Murder.'

THIRTEEN

As Jaxx was tapping away at the console learning every inch of the navigational array, Molly pressed Syl'Va to continue his story.

"How long ago did Lu'Thar capture Torath?" she asked.

Syl'Va thought about it for a moment.

"I wasn't present when he captured your friend. I was on a rescue mission for one of our officers who had been captured by the Allurians. Thought they could get ransom money from our military. They really are stupid."

"Syl'Va, focus please."

He recognised his digression, apologised and continued.

"From what I gathered, this was the second time Lu'Thar had captured Torath. The first time, I was still at the academy on Deltaria, but your friend escaped using the same tricks he did years before. But this time, he slipped up and trusted a group of Kaleys, who sold him out to the Captain. Lu'Thar has had him chained up in the interrogation room on the *Challenger* since it launched last year, and for at least two years before that on the penal station around our planet. And he isn't using words to extract information."

Molly and Jaxx both shuddered at those words. They both knew there was only one form of interrogation for the Deltarians.

Molly's mind was now racing with the possibilities. If Torath had gone to the Kaleys, he must have needed more technology. If he had been running from Lu'Thar for all those years since she was separated from him, how much further could he have perfected the technology?

"Was there any evidence to suggest the *Trinity* was still in tact?" she asked, enthusiastically.

Syl'Va shook his head.

"He never said a word regarding the ship's survival. But the way he was determined to pursue it, makes me think it is still out there. And now he thinks you know too."

Molly looked over at Jaxx, who held up the transparent computer module containing the supposed location of the mystery Saxon vessel.

"He thinks you know where the ship is, and that's why he wants you so badly. But we have another problem."

"As if we didn't have enough problems already?" she said, becoming more and more exasperated.

"The other problem is somewhat larger," replied Syl'Va.

Molly sat around, looking at both men in turn, waiting for one of them to explain the situation to her. Jaxx was still processing new information in his brain, and wasn't focussed enough to give her even more bad news. When neither person took the initiative, she threw up her hands in protest, and Jaxx finally cleared his mind and volunteered the answer.

"We contacted one of Syl'Va's former colleagues in the neighbouring system to ask if he had heard anything in terms of a Saxon vessel, or anything to do with the Resurrection project."

"And?"

"They said they hadn't, but they had received a report of movement from the far side of the galaxy. Three Vendarian battleships were sent to investigate. They never returned."

A cold shiver went down Molly's spine as she digested the news.

"It seems our antics have alerted the very people we didn't want involved."

Molly looked over at Jaxx, who had now been joined by Syl'Va.

"The Decimators."

Both men nodded, and as Molly turned and looked through the front window of the bridge, she couldn't help but think back to her nightmare, and the days of her experimental weaponry and think to herself how she wished she had never joined the military.

118

RESURRECTION

FOURTEEN

Fay'Lar watched on as her Captain sent the final mounting bolt through the body of his Chief Engineer. She knew that he was to be feared as well as admired, but even in her iron stomach, there were twinges of nausea at the sight of a fully grown man hanging from a wall like some sort of mutilated painting.

"Let this be a lesson to all of you!" bellowed Lu'Thar to the rest of the bridge crew. "If you fail in your duties, you will pay the price!"

He then walked along the rear deck another six feet, before pointing at an empty space on the wall alongside the engineer.

"And this vacant area, will be where I nail that treacherous former first officer of mine when we catch up with him. Now get back to your duties!"

Immediately, the level of fear on the bridge, catapulted the soldiers back to duty. The damage to the *Challenger* had been substantial despite her formidable size and power. And the unexpectedness of it had caused Lu'Thar to seek swift retribution. His engineer was the first head on the chopping block.

The ship had been adrift for eighteen hours before the engines were repaired enough for low speed. That was eighteen hours of ground they had to make up on a ship which was not far from matching

120

their capabilities. Beresian vessels were notoriously fast, and usually well armed. But despite the setback, and the embarrassment suffered by his ship, he still had unwavering faith in the *Challenger*.

"Lieutenant Fay'Lar, please come with me."

Lu'Thar moved through the doorway into his office, and Fay'Lar cautiously followed him inside. She suspected she knew the reasoning, and that she was about to receive the position that she had felt was owed to her following Syl'Va's betrayal. However, there was reluctance in her mind, having seen her commanding officer slip so quickly into pure rage, and the level of the violence he was now capable of. And still, the majority of the crew were unaware of the mission he was attempting to carry out. Nevertheless, she was a military officer, and was duty bound to carry out the orders of her Captain.

"Please, have a seat, Lieutenant."

It was not often that soldiers were seated at a table. The chairs were more often considered a decoration than an accessory. However, as Lu'Thar took his own seat, she felt able to do the same, and joined him at his desk.

"Lieutenant, you witnessed the betrayal of Syl'Va. I wish to ask you… was I too naive with the former Commander?"

Fay'Lar was taken aback by such a relaxed and unusual question for the man she had just seen nail somebody to a wall moments before. She wasn't entirely sure how to answer.

"Sir?" she asked, as it was all she could muster.

"I wonder if I allowed my personal pride at his success blind me to his behaviour. He questioned me and I allowed him to continue in his position. He did it again, and I allowed him to lead the boarding party. And now I face the prospect of having to kill him."

Fay'Lar was unsure of quite how to respond, but she did her best.

"Captain, may I speak frankly?"

Lu'Thar nodded and gestured for her to continue.

"Syl'Va should never have been appointed your first officer. He was brought up in a very different environment from the rest of us. It gave him more of a *human* like mentality."

She cringed at the thought of being as feeble as a human.

"When it came to the big decisions, and the choices that had to be made, he would shy away from it, and try and justify a way out of them. That is not the way of our people. We are people of justice. If a man is guilty, he is guilty. If an order is given, it must be obeyed. Syl'Va lacked that ability."

Lu'Thar pondered the bold response of his security officer.

"So you believe I made a mistake?" he asked, in a calm tone.

Immediately, Fay'Lar panicked internally, and her stomach began to swirl at the thought she may have just spoken so out of turn that it would be her body mounted on the wall next, rather than Syl'Va's.

"No Sir, I merely suggested…"

"Relax Fay'Lar. You are correct. I made an error of judgement not befitting someone of my position, and it shall not happen again. I would like for you to become my new First Officer, but I trust nobody more than you to lead our forces, and so you shall combine this new role with your existing one. We will track down the human, and the traitor side by side, and we shall seek restoration for Deltaria."

Fay'Lar began to feel pride in her chest quashing the nausea in her gut, and stood to prepare for the ceremonious act of receiving a new commission.

"Lieutenant Fay'Lar, you have shown immense courage and capability in performing your duties, and have proven yourself a fine soldier of the Deltarian Military. You are bestowed with the rank of Commander, and receive the responsibilities of First Officer, as of this date."

Lu'Thar reached into his cloak, and removed a dagger. Fay'Lar had seen this act performed at the military academy but had never fully prepared herself for the day when she would have to give a piece of herself for her duties. Literally.

"I give you the task to carry out. I give you the wisdom to complete it. And you give me your loyalty, and your commitment from now until death. Do you accept?"

"I do accept, Captain."

As the blade was plunged down into Fay'Lar's smallest finger, she snapped her eyes shut. The feeling of pain, and the bone splintering brought the nausea back to the surface, and as she opened her eyes again, she saw that the finger was separated, leaving a trail of blood, and a mark in the desk.

Lu'Thar took the finger and placed it inside a chamber he kept in his desk. As he opened it, smoke poured out the side, and as it cleared, four more fingers could be seen, each with ice crystals on the diamond skin. He placed it alongside his own, taken by the High General, but kept on board his own ship as a reminder of his loyalties to the military. He glanced at Syl'Va's severed limb, but did not remove it, and closed the chamber back up, and reached for the tool that would cauterize Fay'Lar's wound.

"Thank you, Commander. Your loyalty means a great deal. And now, I must fill you in on our next course of action."

"Do we have a plan, Sir?" she asked, still wincing with the pain, even though the wound was now sealed.

"We are going after the human woman, and Syl'Va, and we are going to find that ship. If we can get hold of the Saxon technology, then we will be able to save our planet once and for all."

"I have heard there may be a way to save individual members of a species, but an entire physical planet? Is that truly possible?"

"I believe it is. And when we do, we will be heroes of Deltaria and nobody will be able to stand in our way. Nobody."

"I am at your command, Captain."

Lu'Thar smiled, and slammed his fist on the desk.

"Excellent! You may return to the bridge. I want an ETA on how long until we are back to full strength. And tell our new engineer I want that weak spot fixed before our next battle."

"Aye Sir."

Fay'Lar nodded towards her Captain, and left the room.

Lu'Thar opened a drawer in his desk, and pulled out a small device, similar to a locket. He opened it up, to reveal a picture of his lost daughter, smiling as she ran through the waves on Saritone Bay.

"We will see each other again, Narlia. I swear it."

FIFTEEN

Three Days Later

"I WANT THAT SHIP DISABLED!"

The booming voice of the Allurian Captain vibrated the walls of the bridge, and sent the crew scrambling to get to their consoles. Through the long glass window directly at the bridge's head, the *Challenger* was weaving from port to starboard, dodging each shot, and evading their pursuit.

"Sir, their shielding is unaffected. Weapons are having no effect!"

That was not what the Captain wanted to hear.

"I do not want to hear what is not working, I want solutions! NOW!"

As the Captain threw himself into his metal chair, positioned high above the other stations, to signify his superiority over the other officers, he could not understand how such a military advantage they once held, was now all but neutralised at every turn. At one time, they had known their enemies moves before they did. Had far more powerful ships and weaponry. Now, every species was developing a defence against them. They were slipping behind.

126

But right now, the thing that was confusing him, was how the much larger, and tactically superior Deltarian warship was not firing back.

"Analysis of their weapons. Why aren't they returning fire?"

"I do not know, Sir. The dampening field is affecting our sensors."

Again, the *Challenger* weaved between the shots which were now being fired almost constantly by the tactical officer. Finally, the Allurian weapons made contact with the Deltarian hull, and a small explosion lit up their port engine, but appeared to leave no damage other than a scorch mark on the paint.

"Again!" shouted the Captain.

Three more shots landed on the enemy vessel, this time causing visible disruptions in their shielding, before it was strengthened once more.

"I can now read their weapons status, Captain. The brief gap in the shield reveals their entire defensive system is offline. Cause unknown."

"So apart from their flying skills, they are defenceless?"

"It would appear that way, Sir, yes."

The Captain allowed a wry smile to spread across his lips.

"Contact the nearest vessels. Tell them we have a prized target. If they would care to join the attack, the spoils will be shared."

The bridge crew paused, and each of them looked confused.

"We are to split our reward Captain?" The first officer was the only one to speak.

"We will use them to capture the vessel, and then use both ships to blow them apart. I share with no-one!"

The deception seemed to appease the crew. The Allurians were not the most trustworthy species in the galaxy, even amongst each other. But neither were they naive. They knew they couldn't stay caught up with the vessel, so they enlisted help.

Within moments, two more Allurian vessels joined formation with the first, and between the three of them, they bombarded the *Challenger* with disruptor fire and torpedoes. Every shot hit target and with each one, the Deltarian flagship slowed speed.

"Captain! The ship is losing velocity!"

"Excellent! Match their reduction and prepare to board the vessel. Nobody sets foot on that ship until we do."

As the *Challenger* ground to a halt, the three Allurian vessels moved to surround it and continued firing until the shielding was disabled. The Captain of the lead ship got to his feet and began barking orders to his crew once more.

"Align our ship with theirs, and assemble a boarding party of twenty soldiers, and…"

"...Captain!"

The tactical officer bellowed towards his leader in a state of shock. As the Captain and the others turned towards the viewing window, they watched as the *Challenger* began to ripple, like a stone on the water.

"Explain!" shouted the Captain.

"Sir, sensors are reading... nothing. There's nothing there!"

In a state of disbelief, the Captain looked sharply between the window, and his officer, and before their very eyes, the image of the *Challenger* disappeared.

"What is happening?!"

The Allurian ship rocked violently to port, sending two officers hurtling across the deck plate. Another jolt, this time to starboard, and the tactical console exploded in a fireball of glass and wiring. Through the window, the other two Allurian vessels were hit by multiple shots, one of them losing an engine pylon, floating off into space, leaving the ship listing. As the Captain gripped the arms of his chair, and pulled himself up, he glanced forwards as a huge shadow engulfed them and the other ships. It passed over them, until it had cleared all three vessels. It slowly turned back around until it was facing them directly. As the crew of the lead ship watched on, the real *Challenger* fired a barrage of weapons at the other two ships, and blew them apart. Debris, and fire consumed their viewpoint, many of the officers shielding their eyes from the blinding lights, and the horror of hundreds of Allurian soldiers, being blown into the vacuum of space.

As the flames and debris cleared, the Deltarian flagship ceased fire. A notification alerted the communications officer that a message was being received.

"Captain, they are hailing us."

Wiping away a thin line of blood from his forehead, the Captain regained composure and sat himself upright in his chair once more. He maintained his posture, despite clearly suffering from several broken ribs.

"Open a channel."

The window was covered by a vast image from holographic emmiters surrounding it, to project a video feed from the enemy vessel.

"I am Captain Lu'Thar of the Deltarian Flagship *Challenger*. You are outmatched, outwitted and outgunned. You will surrender your vessel and prepare to be boarded."

"I will not pander to cowards! Using lights and trickery to gain victory! We will not surrender to you!"

Lu'Thar shifted in his seat, just enough for the Allurians to see the mangled engineer on the wall, still pinned up behind him. It had the desired effect, and the Allurian Captain's demeanour changed immediately.

"I… I am Captain Dagar, of the Allurian Warship Jaktar. What do you require from us?"

Clearly Lu'Thar was now in complete control. He'd broken their ships, and now their spirits. But he had a plan for these Allurians. Something he felt would give him an edge. If he knew where to look, and if his intuition was correct.

"I have a mission for you, Captain Dagar. How much do you know about humans?"

Clearly confused, Dagar was unsure how to respond.

"Humans? I know very little. Only that they are gone. Along with their world in the Terran System."

Lu'Thar leaned forwards.

"There are humans left, Dagar. And they have access to a technology that people in your government have been trying to secure for years. A technology that can bring back a race of people from the dead."

Dagar let out a loud and hearty laugh. Lu'Thar did not budge.

"You are talking about magic, Deltarian. I did not think you were so gullible to believe such rubbish!"

Again, Lu'Thar did not move.

"Commander Fay'Lar, please teleport the proof to the Allurian vessel."

A flash of light appeared in Dagar's hands, which died away to leave a computer module in his hands. He looked up at the image of Lu'Thar, who simply gestured for him to load the data. Dagar handed the module to his navigation officer, who slipped it into his console. A three-dimensional specification appeared above his console, detailing all of their knowledge and intel on the *Trinity* and the Saxon regeneration chamber.

"What is this?" Dagar asked. He was not quite sure how to comprehend what he was seeing.

"That technology can be yours, Dagar. It will make you rich and powerful beyond your wildest dreams. And I can deliver it to you."

This was not in character for a Deltarian, bargaining with an inferior opponent. Dagar knew there would be a catch, and one which could prove dangerous.

"What do you want from us, Deltarian?"

Lu'Thar leaned back in his chair.

"I want you to travel to the edge of the galaxy, and get somebody's attention for me."

SIXTEEN

Jaxx's demeanour had definitely shifted since the attack on Draylon Prime. And being a trained Deltarian military officer, Syl'Va had noticed it more than Molly. He was skulking around the consoles, excusing himself from the bridge, and not engaging as much with Molly as he had been previously. The initial thought that came into Syl'Va's mind, was that perhaps he had a hidden affection for Molly, but it was now clear it was something else.

As Jaxx excused himself once more from the bridge, Molly took over the navigation console. In front of her, the holographic chart was plotting their route to the next supposed location of the T*rinity*. They were five hours out. This was one of the more recent sightings, and one Molly was a little unsure of. It would take them directly into known hostile space. The fact that they were now in a Beresian ship would quell the suspicion a little, but not entirely, and Jaxx had apparently come up with a way to project Beresian appearances onto their faces during communication. Sounded a little bit out there, but she didn't have any better ideas.

Syl'Va joined her at the front of the bridge, and began to put his interrogation techniques to use.

"So how long have you known Jaxx?" he asked.

"Oh about two weeks now, why?"

"No reason, just curious. You seem to have quite an affinity for each other, so I assumed you had been partners for a while."

Molly chuckled.

"I think affinity is the wrong word. More like mutual appreciation. I tolerate him, he tolerates me."

Syl'Va began to pace around her chair a little.

"For someone who claims to have been a rebel-type character for most of her time in this century, you seem to place a lot of trust in him."

Molly began to feel a little uneasy at these questions, and sensed Syl'Va was building to something.

"Well, he is a bi-product of my people, I mean humans did create his race. Maybe it's a psychological thing."

"Yes, perhaps you're right. It just seems like you have a deeper connection, that's all."

Molly locked the ship into auto-pilot and spun the chair around.

"Just what are you getting at Syl'Va?" she asked, in a much higher and aggravated tone.

Syl'Va's expression however, did not alter.

"I am simply suggesting that you may want to start slipping back into some of your old ways, and ask yourself, on a ship where almost everything can be done from the bridge, where he keeps going."

As Syl'Va returned to the tactical console, and turned his chair around, Molly realised that she hadn't noticed where he was going. She had brushed aside the odd behaviour he had displayed when she was in the medical bay, as they had more pressing matters. But now she was beginning to wonder.

"Why are you so interested in the ongoings of Jaxx, or myself for that matter? I thought you were here to help."

Syl'Va spoke without turning to face her.

"On a Deltarian vessel, there is no room for doubt or secrecy. I found that out the hard way. Given my recent history with Lu'Thar and the crew of the *Challenger*, I figured going back to the old ways would suit us best. Honesty, Molly. That is the best way forward."

Honesty. She thought about that. She hadn't been honest with anyone in a long time, least of all herself. She had learned some very hard lessons in the last seven years. Only she knew the full truth. And of course, Syl'Va was right. She was keeping things from Jaxx. She had learnt during her encounters with Rilan and the Kaleys, that keeping her cards close to her chest was the best way for her to operate. But maybe it wasn't any longer.

"Excuse me for a moment," she asked of Syl'Va, who simply nodded as she stood up and walked over to the doors at the rear of the bridge.

As the doors opened, she stopped in her tracks. Standing in front of her, was Jaxx. He was holding her Saxon rifle at head height, and pointing it directly at Molly.

"What the fuck do you think you're doing!?" she exclaimed.

"Sit down."

"Jaxx, what's going…"

"I SAID SIT DOWN!"

Molly backed away until her backside made contact with the Captain's chair, and she sat down, as ordered, all the while, Syl'Va looking on, surveying the situation. It would appear his suspicions had been correct.

"You lied to me," said Jaxx, clearly upset at the information he had uncovered since boarding this vessel.

"I don't understand, Jaxx. What are you saying?"

Jaxx chuckled, before addressing his next command to the computer.

"Computer, please recount the file on former Beresian prisoner six-four-nine-three-two. In full."

Molly's eyes lowered. She had been afraid of this, when she had chosen the Beresian vessel. She knew it had been a risk, but they had been out of options.

"Prisoner six-four-nine-three-two. Birth name, Molly Coben. Aliases include Molly Greenwood, Amelia Darden, Molly O'Brien and Cassie Richards. Crimes include, but are not limited to treason, assault, theft, criminal damage and first degree murder. Current whereabouts unknown. Prisoner six-four-nine-three-two escaped from the Frankar Penal Colony on the Beresian homeworld three years ago, and has not made contact since. Bounty currently stands at four-million credits. Any persons who should come into contact with this person should consider her armed and extremely dangerous and report it to the nearest authorities immediately."

Syl'Va let out a deep sigh, as Jaxx lowered the rifle slightly. He stood from his console and looked at the two of his companions, and shook his head.

"You are as bad as each other."

Jaxx was caught off guard and even Molly was slightly confused. But Syl'Va elaborated without being asked.

"Computer, please recount the criminal record of Jaxx Dracon. In. Full."

Jaxx lowered the weapon the rest of the way down.

137

"Jaxx Dracon, known to Beresian authorities as former prisoner seven-eight-seven-eight-one. Arrested two years ago for petty theft. Served six months at the Frankar Penal Colony. Was arrested a second time one year ago for attempting to bribe the Chancellor of the Beresian Council. Sentenced to two years in Frankar Penal Colony. However, prisoner seven-eight-seven-eight-one failed to arrive at the colony and was declared a renegade. Bounty currently stands at two million credits."

"I could ask the computer to recount the records from other species' databases if you'd like?" Syl'Va said rather calmly.

Jaxx lay the disruptor down and sat opposite Molly in the science station seat.

"Why didn't you tell me about your past?" he asked, seemingly hurt by having to dig out these details himself.

"Same reason you didn't tell me, I'm guessing," she replied.

"Molly, how can we trust each other, if we keep secrets. This mission may get us all killed. We need to know everything!"

Molly avoided his gaze momentarily, and the thought of what she was still keeping from him. She looked over at Syl'Va, who simply nodded at her, as if telling her to proceed.

"Jaxx, there's more you need to know."

Jaxx looked over at Syl'Va who nodded again. He seemingly knew that more was being hidden. Damn military officers, always interrogating people without even asking a question. That was a skill Jaxx envied greatly.

"When I found you at the bar that night, I wasn't looking for the computer module. Well I was, but I could've taken it earlier in the day from Finbar myself. I was looking for you."

Jaxx was speechless. Up until she had killed the Allurians that night, he had never laid eyes on Molly. How could she know about him?

"Looking for me? Why? How?"

Molly sighed.

"I knew about the Valkor. I knew you were created by humans, but I'd never actually seen one. I needed to know if I could use you."

"Use me? Use me for what?"

This conversation was now getting very uncomfortable for Jaxx, and he was beginning to wish he hadn't put that rifle down.

"Based on Torath's notes, I still believe the Resurrection project pulls genome sequences from your DNA to recreate your ancestors. If that is true, then with your ancestors being human, we could use your DNA to bring some of them back. It would double our efforts."

"But my species were artificially created," replied Jaxx.

"Yes, but the humans used their DNA in the process as a base foundation. There is human in every Valkor. And that's why when I saw you on the wanted list when I snuck aboard Finbar's ship, I knew I had to find you."

Jaxx was trying desperately hard to take in all this new information. He wasn't sure he could trust her any longer. She had known he was a career criminal the whole time, but he had no idea quite how violent and manipulative she had been.

"I suppose all of that nonsense about the Kaleys and Rilan was bull shit too."

Molly's eyes pleaded with him to trust her.

"No! All of that was true! I swear to you Jaxx, I never intended to mislead you, but my priority is to bring back humanity from the dead. I have to do this, by whatever means are needed. *Whatever means.* Do you understand that?"

Jaxx had begun to realise that there was a darker side to Molly. Something was propelling her to do this. More than simply being the last of her race, but something *deeper* within her.

"I understand you need to bring them back. But why you specifically? Why are you so hell bent for *you* to be the one to do it?"

Molly burst forward out of the chair, and Jaxx leaned towards her, and grabbed her arm to stop her. She tried to push him away, but he

140

intensified his grip. Molly swung her other arm across his jaw, knocking him to the floor. Syl'Va did not interfere. As Jaxx picked himself up off the deck, he charged at Molly, who delivered another punch to his jawline, followed by a swift kick to the abdomen.

Again, he charged towards her, and grabbed her shoulder, and this time she delivered four punches to his gut, one swift lash across the face, and picked him up, swung him over her shoulder, and slammed his body down onto the communications console, shattering the display and sending sparks shooting out of the sides, the noise only deafened by the sound of several of Jaxx's vertebrae breaking on impact.

She lunged towards his deflated body, and wrapped her hands around his elongated neck and applied pressure, tears filling her eyes. As the life was gradually being choked out of him, Jaxx managed the question he had been trying to ask.

"What… did… you… do…?"

Molly's grip intensified, until Jaxx's breath was almost ceased, and then she realised what she was doing, and let go, her hands recoiling at the imagery of what she had done. Jaxx let out garbled coughs and spluttered in an effort to increase his intake of oxygen.

"I… I… started it all."

141

RESURRECTION

SEVENTEEN

**Four years earlier**

The library was quiet. The timing was perfect. Nobody would notice her slipping in through the back door at this time of night. The only people who tended to frequent the place this late were students, and Molly couldn't see any of those around.

As she gently closed the door behind her, she made her way towards the archives. Brief sounds of movement from the front desk caused an instinctive reaction for her to slink back into the shadows, but it as simply the clerk placing documents back into his filing cabinet. In many ways this reminded her of the libraries on Earth. Not that she ever had much time to visit them, but she had always adored the smell of old books, and files. Something about it just set of the nostalgia within her, and gave her comfort, in a way nothing else did.

As she positioned herself at one of the interfaces, she reached into her pocket and pulled the Beresian computer module out that she had stolen from one of the administrators that morning. As she placed it into the interface, it overrode the login screen and allowed her access with very little effort. Rilan had always tried to keep her in the dark about anything to do with the Decimators, but she had to know why Earth was targeted. She had carried this guilt for over two hundred years. Even as she was in cryogenic suspension, she had brief flashes of images in her mind of her causing the planet's destruction. If it was true what people said about them wiping out those they considered lesser species, then there would be no issues. But she couldn't shake the guilt she had nursed since the attack. She had to know one way or the other.

News article after news article moved across the screen. Evidence of Deltarian military strikes being covered up to protect the High General from prosecution, the assassination of the Vandarian Prime Minister by a rogue Allurian commander, the last recorded death of a Saxon elder. And then it appeared. The attack on Earth. The Beresians kept an immaculate record of everything they came across, and were known to have eyes across the galaxy. The Kaleys that had held Molly captive, often spoke about them having spies everywhere, and sticking their noses where they didn't belong. If the Saxons had been watching Earth, then it was only reasonable that other species had been too. But it wasn't news reports that she was searching for. It was military records, and scientific anomalies.

She punched in a few commands into the search function, and each time a security access request appeared, the little computer module flashed and entered the information for her. And then she found it. A report from the Beresian research station Gamma-Six.

"Energy weapon displacement detected on Terran homeworld. Further investigation required. Recommend military investigation."

144

That was the complete report. *Energy weapon displacement.* Molly cycled back to the top of the document to find the date, and there it was.

"February 16th 2152."

That was the first day her weapon had been tested in Plymouth. That test completely obliterated a warehouse with a single shot. And that was the day she had started to wonder what she had done. She needed more. The search continued, and she found further records from the research station.

"July 9th 2154.

Reported increase in weapons activity on Terran homeworld. Movement detected in Scandarian system at similar time. Monitoring is urgently required. Beresian militia has been notified."

And another.

"September 6th 2155.

Several increased weapons testing has been detected in upper atmosphere of Terran homeworld. Initial scans appear to show the indigenous species, known as humans, are preparing to arm themselves against outer threats. Further movement detected in neighbouring system by unknown vessel. Ship not responding to enquiries. Militia sent to investigate, but communications failed."

As the horror truly began to set in to Molly's brain, she read the final two reports.

"31st October 2155.

Unknown vessel entered star system of human planet. Communications have been unsuccessful. Militia sent to intercept, but all ships destroyed. Vessel appears to be responding to proposed weapons testing."

"3rd November 2155.

Human homeworld has been destroyed. Unknown craft descended into planet's atmosphere, and opened fire using unknown weapons technology. No known survivors. Gravity fields have been destabilised across entire region, and planets are falling out of alignment. Ship has now left the Terran system. Queries have revealed this unknown vessel may belong to the secretive species known only as The Decimators. No further weapons activity detected."

Molly logged herself out of the archives, and removed the computer module, placing it back in her pocket, before covering her eyes with her hands. That was it. Her suspicions had been confirmed. Despite the theories that the Decimators only annihilated lesser species than themselves, they had been attracted to Earth by her weapons testing. She was responsible.

Her mind was now closed to all possibilities other than one. She *must* find Torath, and the *Trinity*. They were both out there

146

somewhere, and she needed to find them. She had to repair what she had done. And nothing and nobody would stop her. She would resurrect the human race.

At any cost.

RESURRECTION

EIGHTEEN

"Well, Commander. I would say that the tests of the new holographic combat systems have gone extremely well. What is next?"

Fay'Lar checked through her duty roster, as she took a sip from her drink, sitting very assuredly, with a newfound confidence after her first tactical development as First Officer.

"We have another round scheduled for tomorrow morning, and then minor modifications to make to the shuttle craft to allow them to interact with the holographic ships during intense and wide ranging combat. Essentially, they will know which ships are fake, but the enemy will not."

Lu'Thar let out quite a belly laugh, considering the way his life had gone recently.

"Excellent! Fay'Lar, I should have made you my right hand woman years ago. The advances you have made in just six days in your new role have surpassed what our military developers have achieved in twelve months. You are an invaluable asset."

The two held up their glasses in triumph, before downing their entire contents. However, the dinner was interrupted by the second officer.

149

"Lieutenant Moltar to Captain."

"Go ahead Lieutenant."

"Apologies for interrupting Sir, but I think you and the Commander should come to the bridge."

"What is it Lieutenant, spit it out."

"Apologies Captain, but you really do need to see this for yourselves."

The comm line went dead, and the two officers exchanged glances, before rising from the table and heading for the bridge. As they rounded the corner, and the doors to the bridge opened before them, they both stopped in the doorway. Displayed on the viewing screen at the head of the room, was a Saxon vessel.

"Report. What am I looking at Lieutenant?"

Moltar entered several commands, unsure how to confirm it himself, but his reply was the same as the displayed result had shown him now three times.

"It is a Saxon preservation vessel, Captain."

Fay'Lar moved forward to take her position alongside the Captain's chair, before continuing the scan from her personal console.

"Scans show three lifeforms aboard, Captain… all Saxon."

Lu'Thar sat himself slowly down in his chair.

"The vessel. What is its designation?"

The image on the viewing window zoomed in on the Saxon vessel's hull until a registry could be seen etched below the right hand side of the cockpit window.

"The vessel is identifying as the *Horizon,* Captain."

This name did not mean anything to Lu'Thar, or his second officer. However, Fay'Lar remained rigid in her seat. Noticing her restraint, Lu'Thar turned to his First Officer.

"You know this vessel, Fay'Lar?"

She nodded.

"Do enlighten me, Commander."

Fay'Lar remained silent briefly, before being prodded by her superior again.

"Commander?"

"The Horizon is the vessel that murdered my family, Captain."

RESURRECTION

NINETEEN

The space in this region seemed even blacker than usual. There was a distinct lack of stars, and there had been no planets for two days anywhere within sensor range. It was as if the Allurian vessel *Jaktar* was moving through some kind of void.

Captain Dagar was feeling something he had not felt in quite a while. *Fear.* He knew what lived in this region of space, and he and his species had only ever ventured here once before. On the promise of profit and technology beyond their wildest dreams, a small fleet of Allurian warships had headed here to claim such a prize. Only three escape pods made it back to their territory, aboard one of which was a young Field Ensign Dagar.

"Sensors?"

"Nothing, Sir. No readings of any kind."

"Confirm we are still at high velocity?"

"Confirmed Captain. There just isn't anything out here."

Dagar slammed his fist on his command console, the display fritzing momentarily from the impact. Why was he on such a foolish mission without reassurances? He had never gone *knowingly* into such danger for a myth. He was doing his best to hide his anxiety from the rest of the crew, as displaying it before

153

them would be seen as a weakness. But his resilience was wearing thin.

"Full alert!" he ordered. "This doesn't feel right, and we will not be ambushed in the dark like some Deltarian mine dwelling mole!"

The weapons officer acknowledged the order, and raised all shielding to its maximum level, and placed all weapons on standby.

"If there is something hiding in the shadows, we will be ready!"

The crew began to shift uncomfortably at their stations. They were not as well experienced as their Captain, and many had only been aboard the Jaktar for a matter of months. The pilot was the first to crack under the pressure.

"Captain, do you not think this a foolish mission? We do not know what is out here, and we have no promises on our prize at the end if we are even successful. Furthermore we…"

The shot was almost pin point between the ribs, striking the heart of the pilot directly. A splatter of dark crimson blood sprung outwards from the wound, as the pilot fell forward, the look of surprise still etched on his now dead face. Dagar placed his disruptor back into its holster, and sat back down.

"Dispose of that."

"Aye Sir!"

"And get me another pilot. One who can keep his mouth shut."

As the pilot's body was dragged from the bridge, leaving a smear of blood along the deck plating as he went, Dagar swore that he had seen movement through the viewing window. His eyes narrowed and his glare intensified, focussing on the blackness being displayed before him.

There! Another movement. Almost like a ripple in a placid lake of water. Another! Something was definitely moving out there, and making just enough distortion to be visible at certain moments.

"Lieutenant, sensor readings now?"

"Still negative, Captain."

"But there is something moving out there!"

The remaining bridge crew began to join their Captain in staring out into the void.

"There! You see it?" Dagar exclaimed excitedly.

None of the crew confirmed it, but they all continued to look.

"Over there Captain!" exclaimed the new pilot, as he slumped into the seat of its former occupant.

"And there, Sir!" shouted the weapons officer.

And then, the operations console began bleeping, and flashing some kind of warning. The Captain turned to look towards his officer, and was greeted with a very confused look.

"Report!"

"Captain, someone is downloading our flight data, and our mission logs."

Dagar's eyes bulged with surprise. Their shielding was at maximum, so how could anything penetrate that simply for data retrieval?

"How is that possible?" he exclaimed.

The operations officer simply shook his head.

"I do not know Sir, but now our personal logs are being taken, and all of our communications records. It's as if someone is trying to see what we are doing here, where we have come from, and who we have spoken to… without bothering to ask us."

Dagar's fear and anxiety had now turned to rage. How dare an unannounced aggressor hack into his ship and take what was his. Despite knowing the danger of this territory, he embraced his inner fighter.

"Enough of this outrage! Prepare four torpedoes, and target them at each point of the compass. We will stand our ground and stop these snakes from taking our information!"

"Captain?"

"Do you have a problem with your orders?!"

"Captain! Our weapons are offline!"

A swirling vortex began forming in the pit of Dagar's stomach.

"WHAT?!"

"Weapons are down, Sir, and… Sir! Shields have just failed!"

"WHAT IS HAPPENING?!"

As Dagar spun back around to look out of the viewing window, a small glimmer of green light could be seen sparkling in the distance. As his eyes once again squinted to gain better focus, the twinkling became more prominent against the black backdrop, glowing brighter, and getting bigger. The rest of the bridge crew also were now captivated by this glowing green light in the middle of nothing but darkness.

But as it grew closer, the reality dawned on Dagar. This was not a twinkling light. He slumped back down in his chair, gazed at his control panel, which displayed that all main power was now somehow offline, reiterating the fact that his ship was totally defenceless, and took a deep breath.

As the single twinkling light split into six twinkling green lights, the crew began to run and scramble back towards their stations, but Dagar simply closed his eyes. All six torpedoes hit the Jaktar simultaneously, causing a cascade reaction along the outer hull until the inner hull began to buckle too. Explosion after explosion ripped through the ship, until the entire vessel was blown apart by one final eruption.

The light from the flames briefly lit up the silhouette of a large black mass moving towards it, slowly. As the explosions came to an end, and the debris stopped glowing, the darkness returned. The only evidence that a vessel was still in the area, was the sudden change in direction of some of the debris pieces, as they bounced off the black hull.

TWENTY

Molly and Jaxx had barely spoken for the last three days. Since her revelation that she believes it was her weapons research that seemed to attract the Decimators to Earth, she had withdrawn into herself. She was ever present on the bridge, making course corrections, preparing the ship for battle, but in terms of socialising, this had become non-existent.

Jaxx had become very fond of Molly, and having a genetic connection to her, he felt like he should be doing something to help, but he just couldn't find the words. How does one console somebody for potentially destroying their entire race? After all, it had blown open the idea and believed motives of these powerful creatures. They not only extinguished species they deemed as 'lesser' but those they also deemed as a potential threat.

Syl'Va on the other hand, had spent those last few days being very productive, teaching Jaxx about the capabilities of the *Challenger*, and attempting to upgrade their own defences should they encounter Lu'Thar again any time soon. His latest modification was almost ready.

"Jaxx, Molly, may I please have a moment? I have something to show you."

159

Without speaking, the two of them approached the tactical console, and awaited Syl'Va's demonstration.

"The *Challenger* is equipped with a vast array of weaponry, and shielding, as we know. However, they also have the capability to produce holographic representations of their own vessel in order to lure out an enemy, without directly engaging them in combat."

Jaxx looked surprised.

"Wow, what genius came up with that idea?" he asked.

Syl'Va's enthusiasm was lessened at the sound of Jaxx's.

"It was the warped brain child of Lieutenant Fay'Lar, but never actually put into practice. However, as I am presuming she has now taken my place, I'm under the impression that she will have convinced Lu'Thar to go ahead and make the necessary adjustments."

Molly watched the screen intensely as it demonstrated a simulation of how the system would work.

"So if they have that ability, can we defend against it?" she asked, speaking the most words she had said in three days.

Jaxx smiled at the sound of her voice, and then gave himself a confused expression at how much he had missed hearing it, without realising.

"We can now."

Jaxx smiled, and turned and smiled at Molly, who smiled back. Again, another warm feeling in Jaxx's chest at that smile.

"Go on, Syl'Va."

"Well, I have diverted the energy from the food dispensers, and all but three of the remaining teleportation discs into the forward disruptor cannon. Essentially, we can fire a single shot of the matter energy into space when we encounter the *Challenger,* and it will rebound any holographic images, into images of us instead. Basically, if they generate a hologram of their ship, it will automatically trigger a hologram of our ship in response."

"That is a very clever trick, Syl'Va. Nice work."

Molly was feeling much better. Her task was back on track, and they had a defence against their second biggest threat. The main threat however, she hoped was still lurking in the darkness out of sight and out of mind.

"So how long until we reach the next sighting of the *Trinity*?" asked Jaxx.

Molly looked over at her console before responding.

"Approximately two hours."

An alert from the console, suggesting a proximity alarm.

"But right now, we have bigger problems."

161

As the three of them looked out of the window, four ships began to slowly overtake them, before moving down to box them in.

"Who the hell is that?" Jaxx demanded, rushing to the pilot chair, relieving Molly, who assumed the Captain's chair.

"No ships like this on records," replied Syl'Va.

Molly didn't recognise them either, but whoever they are, they were reducing speed, forcing them to do the same.

"Computer," she asked. "Can you identify the vessels surrounding the ship?"

A momentary pause, and the audible sound of mechanical cogs whirring away.

"The ships do not match any configuration on record, however, they do seemingly contain aspects from other known vessels."

"Elaborate."

"The weapons systems are of Saxon origin. The propulsion systems share the same signature and composites as a Deltarian mining vessel. And the communications array is of Valkorian design."

Jaxx looked up at the sound of his species. Valkorian design? He hadn't been aware that any Valkor had left their planet. Which meant if he was right, somebody must have taken their technology following their evacuations.

162

"How is that possible?" he asked, still in awe at how randomly put together these vessels seemed to be.

"I don't know, but clearly they want us to stop. They're closing within very short distance from the hull. If we don't stop soon, we'll hit them."

Syl'Va suggested opening communications, but they received no response. As Jaxx complied with Molly's suggestion, they dropped out of high speed, and came to a stop, still surrounded by the mysterious vessels. Once they had come to the complete halt, they received a communication.

"Well, I guess they couldn't concentrate on piloting and talking at the same time," quipped Jaxx, who Molly admitted to herself, had finally got his sense of humour back.

"Open the channel Syl'Va."

They were not prepared for the face they were to see on the other side of the screen.

"Hello. My name is Jack Slater. I imagine you have a lot of questions for us."

The man on the screen, was around six-feet-three-inches, with medium length wavy brown hair, and a piercing set of blue eyes. But the main element of his appearance that was causing shock and silence between the crew, was his species.

Jack Slater was human.

RESURRECTION

TWENTY-ONE

Fay'Lar slammed her fist down onto the table with such violent force, that a huge crack appeared down the middle. It was the first time that her anger had truly been demonstrated to Lu'Thar outside of a battle scenario.

"I DEMAND TO KNOW WHERE THEY ARE!" she hollered at the Saxon group sat opposite her.

The lead representative held his hands up for calm.

"If we knew where they were, we would tell you, Commander. This is why we have come to you for help. These renegades must be stopped at all costs!"

Lu'Thar had adopted a relatively calm demeanour compared to his usual style. He had created such an elaborate plan for this mission, and yet he hadn't forseen this element. The re-emergence of a group of people believed to be extinct, on a ship from Fay'Lar's past. He allowed the debate to continue for a little longer before stepping in.

"Commander, please, restrain yourself and allow our guests to make their case."

Fay'Lar shot him a look full of fury, before remembering her place, and taking her seat, albeit reluctantly.

"Please, Reyton, continue."

The lead Saxon stood from his chair and walked over to the monitor displaying the schematics of the *Challenger*. He tapped several commands into the screen, and the vessel's details were replaced by those of his own vessel.

"We are what is left of a small group of Saxon elders, which has been residing on the far side of a neighbouring system, beyond the Granobulen Nebula."

"Which system?" Fay'Lar interrupted.

"I am not prepared to share that information as of yet, Commander. We still have numbers there, and I will not put them in any more danger than I have to."

Reyton was stern in his reply, and was backed up by nodding of agreement from his associates. He continued.

"Six years ago, we were attacked by an unknown assailant. One small scout ship, matching our own designs. We received no communications from the vessel, and had no indication of who was on board. Following the attack, we lost twenty three of our brothers and sisters. The ship then left the system."

"What were they targeting?" Lu'Thar asked.

"Their attack was fairly sporadic, but they did have repeated strikes on our research facility. I believe you are aware of the Resurrection Project, Captain?"

"I believe half of the galaxy now knows of that project. And I am sure you are aware that several other factions are searching for this technology, besides us."

"I am."

Lu'Thar glanced over at Fay'Lar, who was clearly not interested in the Resurrection project and wanted answer about her family and their demise. He gestured for Reyton to continue.

"We believe the assailant was trying to determine the location of the technology. They failed, because we do not have access to it. We never did."

An expression crossed Lu'Thar's face that none of his crew had seen before. A look of unexpected surprise.

"I can tell from your expression Captain Lu'Thar, that you did not expect me to reveal that piece of information."

Lu'Thar shook his head.

"Well, I am sure you are more than aware of the stubbornness of a certain Torath?"

Again, a look of surprise on the Deltarian Captain.

"I take that as a yes. Considering, I know he is currently hanging in your interrogation room."

Fay'Lar this time interrupted.

"How can you know that? Our shields are the strongest in the quadrant! How can you…"

"Commander, please allow me to finish. We do not have time for interruptions."

Fay'Lar sat back down, now matching the surprise being expressed by her Captain.

"Torath is a renegade, Captain. He and his brother broke away from the Saxon council a very long time ago. Roughly around the time he became involved with you, I believe. The Saxon people over the centuries have become renowned for collecting specimens of extinct species, and then preserving them for study. At no point, did the Saxon council ever decide to begin playing God. Torath, however, was adamant he could bring these species back from the brink of extinction. He believed he could use the DNA codes from the specimen, to bring back that individual's ancestors. A genetic time machine if you will. He brought his findings to the council, but we rejected them out of hand. The idea was not only seemingly impossible, but against our beliefs. That is when the Decimators came into the equations."

This time, Lu'Thar spoke.

"The Decimators? You have had direct contact with them? How?"

Reyton looked over to one of his colleagues, and gestured for them to answer the question.

"The Decimators, Captain, are humans."

The Saxon allowed that statement to sink in amongst those in the room.

"That isn't possible."

Fay'Lar was the first to voice any response to the incredible accusation from the Saxons that humans had destroyed their own planet.

The third Saxon, then stood to continue the explanation.

"The humans came to us following the initial attack on our colony. As I am sure you can appreciate, we were convinced they had been dead for over two hundred years, so imagine our surprise when a huge black ship appeared in orbit, and immediately rendered our defences useless. And imagine, our horror, at the tale they told us."

Peyton then altered the image on the monitor to display the design of the Decimator vessel. The details were immense, and had never been seen by the Deltarians before. Or anyone else for that matter. Nobody had ever gotten close enough to their ships to capture such a goldmine of information.

"This is the schematic of their lead ship, the *Vanguard*. They have three ships in total. In. Total. They are not a species of unimaginable power. They are a group of humans, from the future."

Lu'Thar had decided he couldn't listen to any more without making a few things clear.

169

"You expect me to believe that humans, from the future, have come back in time, to wipe out their own people from existence? Why? What is their purpose? How far in the future? How did they gain the technology? Why did they come to you?"

Fay'Lar also joined in with the quick fire questioning.

"And where are the people who destroyed my home, and my family, aboard that very ship you have piloted here? Give me one reason why I shouldn't blow that craft out of the sky, and eject you out of the nearest airlock?"

Reyton once again held his hands high asking for calm. A gesture which was beginning to wear very thin with his hosts.

"Please, I will explain, if you will allow me to finish!"

The Deltarian crew took their seats once more, now more agitated than they had been up to now, and their patience was running out. They were a species of action takers, not diplomats. Long explanations were not something they were used to. However, they needed this information, and so allowed Reyton to continue his long tale of incredible events.

"The crew are Captained by a man called Jack Slater. He and his fellow humans were involved in a colonisation project in the year twenty-nine-sixty-three. Their vessels were constructed to safely transport human populations away from Earth, to suitable locations where they could rebuild and develop. Earth in this time was a barren wasteland, caused by their failure to prevent climate change

170

despite the hundreds of years of warnings by their scientists. In true human fashion, they acted too late. The problem was, as the humans began to spread and grown once again in their new settings, they began to develop a superiority complex. They had access to areas of the galaxy they had never known, and technology of other neighbouring species they had never seen. They wanted it for themselves. Systematically, the humans began to take what they wanted from these peoples, and spread fear throughout the galaxy. Eventually, the death tolls caused from their invasions numbered over one billion. They destroyed entire species. Beresians. Allurians. Valkor. Vendarians. And the Deltarians."

This time, Lu'Thar slammed his fist onto the table, which deepened the crack caused by his Commander thirty minutes before, and the entire table collapsed into the middle in two halves.

"Are you telling me, the Humans destroyed half the species in the galaxy, including noble Deltarians, to quench their thirst for power?"

Reyton nodded. He typed in more commands, and a series of logs and mission reports began appearing on the screen. It was evidence. Legitimate evidence, documenting the events he had described. Even video recordings of planets collapsing in on themselves. The final video record was of a Decimator ship moving away from an imploding Deltaria. Lu'Thar collapsed into his seat.

"You see, Captain. Your planet was still alive and well, five hundred years from now. You have been fed lies by Torath, through

171

hear say, and nonsense from numerous other sources. The humans, led by Slater, could not live with what his race had done. They came across a people, known as The Redemption. They were a group of individuals from many species across the universe that had come together to develop some form of time travel. They wanted to go back in time, in order to correct mistakes that had been made, and save their own individual species. By the time they achieved this goal, the humans were closing in. They had learned of the technology, and wanted to steal it in order to go back in time, not to save their own world, but to be able to dominate other worlds with their superior technology. When Jack Slater learned of this, he put together a crew of one hundred, took the three largest colony ships, and took the technology for himself. He realised humanity could not be allowed to rule the galaxy. The cost was too great. So he took the technology, and went back in time, where he destroyed his own planet, and all of the people on it. With that task done, he then travelled across the galaxy, eliminating any colony, or planet that contained any evidence of human life, colonies, or technology. When he was done, he and his crew retreated into the far reaches of the galaxy out of history's way."

"Why did they not destroy themselves, to completely eliminate the threat of history repeating itself?" asked Fay'Lar. "Or for that matter, simply cease to exist. If there were no humans to continue, how were they still there?"

"That isn't how time travel works," replied Reyton's first colleague.

"If you travel into the past, that then becomes your future. Your existence is not defined by what you do in the past. It simply creates alternate realities. If you kill your parents in the past, you will still exist. You will have simply created an alternate timeline where your alternate self will never be born."

After the rather quick lesson in quantum physics, Lu'Thar decided it was time for decisions to be made. His original plan seemed to be inconsequential now. There was much more at stake than he had first realised. Deltaria did not require saving. The planet would be fine. His daughter was still at the front of his mind, but he now had to evaluate whether one person was worth risking the humans repopulating and destroying all Deltarian life, not to mention other species. Had he been so consumed by his own gains for the last twenty years that he had become as bloodthirsty as the humans in Reyton's tales? Perhaps it was time for a new mission.

"They remained, I imagine, just in case they had failed, and any humans were found to be still living somewhere," Lu'Thar offered up.

Reyton nodded in agreement.

"And this is when they came to us. They had heard rumours that there was a human still alive, and that Saxons were assisting them with the Resurrection project. As it turned out, it had been that

173

human who had attacked us in one of our own vessels. Slater explained that they couldn't risk getting involved, and that we had to deal with Torath ourselves. If we failed, then we would risk being their next target. We had already been victims to their collateral damage and were under no illusions of their powers. We agreed to hunt down Torath, and destroy the technology he was attempting to perfect. However, before we could launch, the scout ship *Horizon* returned and destroyed our shipyard, and killed over half our population. Our research station near the Cassar Deltarian colony confirmed the ship then attacked the settlement, killing all those living there, in order to take components from their scientific facilities to aid the construction of the regeneration chamber."

Fay'Lar finally had her answer. Her family had been decimated for machine parts. Her rage was far from tempered. Now she knew that they had died for nothing. Lu'Thar sensed something in her was building, so he reached his hand out to ease her down a little, while he clarified some further details.

"How did you get the *Horizon* back?" he asked.

"We very nearly blew her apart. We had only three ships left after the attack, and all our resources were going to rebuilding our settlement. However, on a supply run, we came across *Horizon* and we engaged her in battle. We lost one of our ships, but we crippled *Horizon* and the human was forced to bail out. We lost sight of her, but we reclaimed the vessel."

"You were not able to pursue the human?" asked Lu'Thar.

Reyton shook his head.

"Our resources are limited. We are the last of our kind. Our priority is self preservation. But we had to reach out to you. You are the most powerful people besides the Decimators this side of the galaxy. We need your help. Not only for our sake, but for the sake of Deltaria, and all the other worlds that will be at risk if the human and Torath complete their plan."

For the first time, Lu'Thar let out a chuckle.

"Torath will not be completing anything. He is in no fit state to function, let alone build a machine capable of bringing a race back from the dead."

Reyton did not share his levity.

"Captain. You are assuming two things. One. That he has not already completed the technology and has simply hidden it. Which the human woman is now trying to find."

Fay'Lar interrupted.

"And two?"

This time Reyton did let out a laugh.

"Two? Well that's obvious. You're assuming the man you have in custody, actually is Torath."

RESURRECTION

TWENTY-TWO

Molly, Jaxx and Syl'Va were all transfixed on the image before them. None of them could believe what they were seeing, but there it was. Humans. Not *a* human, but *humans*.

"Well? Are we going to talk?" asked Slater.

Molly was the first to react. It had put her off stride completely. She knew what her mission was, but now, she was in unplanned territory.

"How are you here?" she managed to ask, in a hushed voice.

Slater laughed.

"Oh, I'm sure we can all discuss this in person. If you'll just let us aboard our ship, we can…"

Syl'Va cut him off.

"You will not be boarding this vessel, Mr Slater. You clearly have an ulterior motive, or you would not have surrounded us, and then diverted conversation towards coming aboard. That suggests to me that you are hiding something."

Slater's friendly demeanour evaporated quickly. Jaxx on the other hand shot Syl'Va an impressed look, and received a look of acceptance in return.

177

"Listen, Deltarian, we are offering you the courtesy of meeting with us under your terms. We can do this the easy way, or the hard way. Whichever choice you go for, we will be coming aboard your ship."

Molly's defensive instincts kicked in at last.

"Like my security officer says, what are you hiding Slater?"

The humans on screen were now moving swiftly behind him, and it was clear they were about to take action. Jaxx, spotted this and began entering commands in the console next to him.

"Little miss, you have no idea who you're dealing with. We know what you are up to, and we aren't going to allow you to proceed."

For the first time, Molly was disarmed. She knew exactly what her plan was, but the others didn't. She couldn't risk revealing her plan to Jaxx and Syl'Va. She needed them. Luckily for her, she didn't need to come up with an excuse. A short beep from the console behind her, where Jaxx was standing, was followed moments later by the image of Slater violently jarring to one side.

"Oh so that's where the backup weapons systems are!" exclaimed Jaxx.

Syl'Va looked a little confused that he had been bypassed, but again, a slightly impressed look was exchanged between the two of them, joined by a smile from Molly.

"You realise, you can't win this?" Slater claimed.

Molly nonchalantly turned, and strolled back to her Captain's chair, sat down and crossed her legs. An assured grin crept across her face. Jaxx found this very exciting.

"Oh, shit, she's doing a Janeway!" he exclaimed.

Syl'Va was confused.

"What is a Janeway?" he asked.

Jaxx was bouncing with all of the pop culture references running through his brain. He was actually about to live a classic sci-fi battle. Molly addressed Slater again.

"Either you move your vessels out of our way, or we will go through them on our way out."

Slater laughed at that claim. Syl'Va was scrambling to ensure all shielding was up, as he had no idea what Molly was planning. Jaxx, however, was already back at the helm, and preparing for a lateral run straight through the centre of the ships.

"You expect to beat four ships, with our technology and crew? There are three of you on one ship!"

"I don't know where you came from, Mr Slater, and frankly I don't care. You are, however, in my way."

"You know why I am here. And we cannot let you proceed."

"Mr Syl'Va, cut the line."

179

Syl'Va disconnected the communication, and Slater's face vanished from the screen. All the while, Jaxx was bouncing in his seat with excitement.

"Before we do this, can I get you a coffee?" he asked Molly, desperate she would get his reference.

Molly smiled.

"No thank you, Mr Jaxx. I'm sure I'll find coffee in a nebula later."

Jaxx's head was prevented from imploding with childish glee, only by the impact of weapons fire on the ship. As they watched, the four mixed technology vessels began swarming across their path, bombarding them with weapons fire.

"Jaxx, get us out of here! Syl'Va, fire all weapons!"

Their crisp, shiny Beresian vessel was now attempting to weave through the beams of fire, but the coordination of these vessels was simply unbelievable. As good as Jaxx was at piloting, he was extremely outmatched. His excitement at slipping classic *Star Trek* references into a real world situation has now gone. He wasn't even contemplating how they were fighting other humans, when Molly was meant to be the last one left. Right now, he was focussed on escaping. Another barrage of hits to the rear of the ship, and they finally began taking damage.

"Shielding is down to sixty-five percent."

"Can we reinforce it?"

"Negative. We have no additional power without taking it from the weapons or the engines."

Jaxx was now beginning to realise he wasn't in a TV show, he was fighting for his life, and becoming overwhelmed.

"I can't shake them off! They're using tactics I've never seen before, like they know where I'm going to go!"

Several more impacts rocked the ship.

"Shielding down to thirty-two percent. We can't take much more of this, Molly."

Molly remained in her seat, stern faced, watching the action unfold on screen. She couldn't come this far and give in. But she needed a plan. If Slater captured her, then everything would be over.

"Open communication with Slater."

Jaxx and Syl'Va looked at each other.

"Are you sure?" Jaxx asked.

"Just do it!" she screamed, as sparks exploded from the science station following yet more impacts.

The hits stopped, and they watched as the four ships once again closed around them, sporting almost no damage from their return fire.

Once again, Slater appeared on the screen.

181

"You have finally decided to listen?" he asked, with an air of smugness about him.

"You haven't left us much choice."

Molly's reply was cold, but calculating. Her eyes were working fast, to match her brain. She was saying one thing, but planning another. Jaxx had seen that look before. And he didn't like it.

"Very well. Lower your remaining shielding and prepare to be boarded."

The screen went blank, and Jaxx made his move.

"You're not planning a repeat of the whole Cliff scenario are you?" he asked sheepishly.

Molly ignored him, and made a line for the rear of the bridge. Tapping several commands into the wall panel near the doors, a hidden compartment opened up, inside of which was a series of rifles and disruptors.

"How did you know that was there?" asked Syl'Va.

No answer.

"Molly?" asked Jaxx.

After tapping the power settings up to maximum, she gripped her rifle tightly. She closed her eyes, took a deep breath and spun on the spot. As she pulled the trigger, a bolt of bright green launched its way across the bridge, and burned a hole right through the centre of Syl'Va's chest. As he fell forwards, out of his chair, a look of shock still on his now dead face, he hit the deck plating with a thud, immediately followed by the sound of his blood dripping from the gaping cavity in his body.

Trembling, as she gripped the rifle so tightly, that her hands had turned white, she turned to aim it at Jaxx.

"Molly! What have you done?" he exclaimed, still not fully processing what he had just witnessed.

"I'm sorry."

There was nowhere for Jaxx to go. His eyes shifted from left to right, the glowing pearl colour widening as he realised he may be about to face death. He closed his eyes, and waited for the inevitable. As Molly went to pull the trigger, a secondary explosion in the science station behind her, knocked her off balance, and as she fired, the beam of energy struck the helm console besides Jaxx, and obliterated it, sending him flying through the air across the bridge, slamming into the screen at the front of the room, which shattered, and Jaxx, and the glass landed on the floor.

As the intruder alarm sounded, Molly knew she was out of time. She looked over at Jaxx, who was covered in glass, blood, and seemingly had severe burns from the explosion. He wasn't moving. She reached into her pocket, and removed a teleporter disc she had been hiding as a backup should she need it. Another glance at Jaxx's limp body, before activating the disc. She melted upwards through the ceiling of the bridge, and headed towards one of the attacking vessels.

The doors to the bridge burst open, and dozens of humans armed with their own rifles crowded the room, followed closely by Jack Slater. He surveyed the room, and his eyes fell upon the dead Deltarian to his left. A tinge of queasiness entered his gut, at he realised he may be too late. Another quick survey of the room, and he spotted Jaxx lying on the ground, and the destroyed navigational console. One of the other humans alerted his Captain to Jaxx's condition.

"Sir, this one is alive."

Slater nodded, and gestured for him to be taken away.

As Jaxx was carried out of the bridge, Slater wandered around the consoles, looking for indications of where Molly may have gone, until he reached the long range sensors. Switching them to short-range, he let out a deep sigh. He was now only reading three of his ships in the area.

The fourth was gone.

TWENTY-THREE

It had been seventy-two hours since the Saxons had left the *Challenger* and Lu'Thar had spent most of that time sat in the interrogation chamber. The now dead body of who he thought was his former ally, Torath, was long gone. Following the revelation from the Saxons that he may not be the true man, he had immediately gone to find out. He questioned the old man, who refused to answer his questions, and when a frustrated blow from Lu'Thar's hand snapped his neck, the body was taken away for examination. It was then that the doctors determined this man was a clone.

All of this meant that Lu'Thar's entire mission, from the loss of his daughter, to building the *Challenger*, to hunting down the regeneration chamber, was now in tatters. None of that mattered. He had been misled by Torath as to the condition of his planet. Something which he now realised in hindsight, had been made obvious when Torath had refused to help him save it using his technology. Torath had simply wanted access to Deltaria's resources to further his research. There was no real friendship there.

He had been consumed by the desire to bring back his daughter, but now he faced an even greater decision. Allow his daughter to rest in peace, or bring her back and risk the extinction of his own race.

185

One thing was for certain. The human woman could not be allowed to locate the real Torath, and his technology.

In the midst of the questioning of his new mission, an irony had not been lost on him. He was the one who had sent the Allurians to lure the Decimators from their space. He knew they would not return, and he also knew the Decimators would learn of their plans. He had intended for this to be a master stroke, and for them to wipe out the human, and Torath, while he snuck in and took the technology. Now, however, he knew that they would prevent the technology being used by any cost, including wiping out anyone in their way. They may be humans, but they were indeed worthy of the name Decimators.

The intercom on the door chimed, and upon hearing his first officer's voice, Lu'Thar ordered her to enter the chamber.

"Captain, we are closing on the location of the firefight we detected last night."

"Early reports?"

"The debris does appear to be from the Beresian vessel the human and the Valkor took from Draylon Prime. However, it appears to be an insufficient quantity for the whole vessel."

"Meaning, they were damaged, but likely escaped."

Fay'Lar nodded.

"There is something else, Sir."

186

Lu'Thar glanced once more at the chains hanging from his ceiling, and the dried green blood on the cuffs.

"And what is that Commander?"

"There are traces of Saxon weapons fire… and Deltarian engine signatures."

That caught Lu'Thar's attention.

"From the same vessel?"

"It would appear so."

Lu'Thar stood to his full height, now towering over Fay'Lar by a clear foot. He walked over to the nearest terminal, and held down the interface button.

"Computer, are there any mentions in the database given to us by the *Horizon* of ships of multiple construction techniques?"

A brief pause and a slew of technical noises as the computer pondered his request.

"Affirmative. The logs of the Horizon indicate that the Decimators acquired several smaller vessels upon their arrival in this time period in order to perform reconnaissance missions undetected. These vessels were then modified using technology from other cultures. However, there is no record of them being used in recent times."

187

Lu'Thar deactivated the wall terminal. No records, until now, he thought to himself. It looks like one way or another, the Decimators were now involved in the situation. And a very delicate situation it had now become. On the one hand, they would be assisting the Deltarians in hunting down the human and her allies. But on the other hand, they didn't care who they had to destroy in order to do it. Whatever their motives, the Decimators surely had to agree they had become the kind of people, they had sought to prevent being born.

"Orders, Captain?"

Lu'Thar snapped out of his deep thoughts. The last three days had changed him irrevocably. He found himself slipping back into the old ways of his people. They used to be the police of the galaxy. Perhaps it was not too late to grab onto those values again. The fate of several species, including his own was at risk. It was time to be a man of integrity once again. His ship was a formidable foe. He was confident of a strong showing in battle with the Deltarians if it came to it, especially with the details given to them by Reyton and his crew. He had made his decision.

"Commander, collect all debris elements and have them placed on the cargo deck, and get the engineering team to examine them extensively. As soon as the fragments are on board, begin tracing the engine signature before it dissipates. We need to find the human before the Decimators do. And my old friend, Torath."

TWENTY-FOUR

The seventeenth punch was now just a dull thud on Jaxx's skin. He had been beaten so many times, the feeling had now gone from his body entirely. His shirt had been torn from his body, and the bruising on his muscular physique was dark and plentiful. There was barely a square inch that had not had injury inflicted on him. He just managed to muster the strength to spit out a mouthful of his own blood, the chains jingling above him, as he swayed.

As Jack Slater placed his hand into a bucket of ice to cool it from the effects of his interrogation, he turned to address the Valkor.

"I have to commend these Deltarians. Their interrogation chambers are quite effective in both design and execution."

Jaxx could not muster much in the way of a response.

"I'm sure you must be bitterly disappointed by your friend's betrayal, but right now all I want is information. I don't understand how that is a difficult request Mr Jaxx."

Jaxx managed to raise his head, and turned to look at Slater, through the one eye which had not yet closed up from the swelling.

"I... don't... know... where... she... is..."

Another shot across the jaw, and more of Jaxx's blood flew across the room and up the adjacent wall. He coughed and spluttered as he struggled to retain consciousness.

"I know that you looked into Ms. Coben's past. The records of your vessel prove that. You know about the Resurrection project and the existence of the regeneration chamber. So I ask you again. Where is she going?"

Jaxx summoned all of his strength, and with every ounce he had left, he bellowed his response.

"I DON'T FUCKING KNOW!"

And with his outburst delivered, he relinquished all of his strength, and simply hung from the chains.

Slater let out a heavy sigh. Whilst it was frustrating that he did not get any information regarding Molly's whereabouts from Jaxx, he knew that he was telling the truth. Her deception for her own crew had more or less proven that. The level of violence she had gone to in order to dispatch the Deltarian Syl'Va was evidence enough of that. The question now remained, what to do with this Valkor. His history showed them to be extinct, and yet in this timeline, it had been him and his vessels that had almost caused their destruction.

Jaxx was one of the last of his kind, which was a recurring theme in Slater's line of work. He had come back to destroy Earth and her colonies to prevent the extinction of these species, and could therefore not contribute to that here.

"You know, Mr Jaxx, I admire your people. I always have. The Valkor were the best of humanity. All of our strengths and none of our weaknesses. I think that is part of the reason your creators and their descendants returned to destroy your race when they realised you were far more advanced. But you must understand, that if we don't find your friend, Molly, all of that may be in jeopardy, and everything we have fought so hard for, will be in vain."

Jaxx, now barely conscious, was beginning to put two and two together. But surely he was wrong. Surely this was not possible. But the more information Slater offered, the more he realised he was right.

"Have you ever watched a planet die, Jaxx? I have. I watched as Earth burnt to a cinder. The oceans, the forests, the deserts, the lush green countryside, and the snowy mountain alps. Watching your planet die is one thing. Having to be the one to push the button makes it impossible to live with. But I did what had to be done. As I did with all those colonies throughout the galaxy."

Jaxx turned his head, his lips trembling, dried blood in the corner of his mouth.

"You're… you… the… Decimators."

Slater shivered at the sound of that name.

"We are humans!" he bellowed. "We did what was necessary, when humanity became too big for its boots, and took ownership of the galaxy! We thought we were gods, and we had a right to whatever

191

we saw. We had access to new technology and planets that we could previously only have dreamed of! We ignored the cries of help from our own planet, and watched it die, before moving on and becoming the worst possible versions of ourselves. At first, it was believed we were saving our race. But the stronger we got, it became evident to me and many of those left that we were condemning the rest of space to insufferable existences. Humanity became the enemy of the galaxy. And I couldn't live with that. And so we took action. Me and my crew are all that is left. And we must finish the task."

Jaxx mouthed more words, as his energy levels rose slightly.

"Molly… bringing… back… humans… Torath…"

Slater nodded, and moved to stand next to Jaxx.

"Yes, Jaxx. She is not the clean cut saviour that you believe her to be. She has killed thousands of innocent people, because she believes it was her fault that Earth was destroyed. Her weapons programme had nothing, absolutely nothing, to do with Earth's demise. There was no target destination for us. We simply activated the technology, and ended up in Molly's time. When we completed our mission, we retreated to the edge of the galaxy, to the void we call home, and entered stasis. Until we were awoken by our systems indicating that a ship had entered range. Once we extracted information from these intruders, and their computer banks, we learned of the potential threat from this Resurrection project, and sought out a group of Saxons, informing them they must put a stop to this project, and deal with this Torath. We then returned to our space. Until we were alerted once again by a small Allurian ship. Their information proved worrying. The Saxons had failed to deal with the threat, and now there was a real danger the project was nearing completion. We needed to act."

Jaxx felt like such an idiot. He couldn't comprehend that one of his ancestors, the people who created his very race, could be capable of such horrors. And yet Molly had betrayed him. Attempted to kill him, in order to get away. And as much as they were making themselves out to be the good guys, these humans were just as bad, if not worse than Molly. Molly was acting on a false guilt, and her own experiences combined with this, had broken her mind. She felt she was doing the right thing. But how far will one woman go to bring back her race from the dead. A race that apparently will destroy billions of innocent lives.

"I will ask you once more, Jaxx. Do you know anything about where Torath and Molly may be? Any indications at all of where the chamber could be concealed?"

Jaxx was about to shake his head in the negative, when he remembered something. An insurance policy he had taken. Molly was not the only one who was always trying to watch her back. In his line of work, it always paid to have some form of leverage.

"My… my… back… pocket… left… side."

193

Slater went to reach into the pocket indicated, but withdrew it, cautiously. He was dealing with a potential enemy, and was almost very naive in his pursuit of answers.

Jaxx however, indicated again.

"My back pocket… computer module… sightings… of the *Trinity*."

Slater now understood, and placing his hand into the pocket described, he withdrew the transparent computer chip that had started Jaxx's entire adventure. Slater immediately moved towards a computer terminal, and slid the chip into the interface. The maps loaded up, now updated with crosses over the failed locations, leaving only one remaining. The final sighting of the *Trinity*.

"Yes! Wonderful! Thank you, Mr Jaxx!"

Slater was now very animated. He had gotten what he wanted from his interrogation. He regretted the violence used in order to obtain it, but the ends to him, justified the means.

"Mr Stevens, please take Mr Jaxx to the medical bay, and repair his wounds. He is to be treated with great care!"

Jaxx was unchained, and four men carried him out of the room, leaving Slater on his own, staring out of the window. The vastness of his ship had always amused him. It dwarfed every other vessel it had ever encountered, and its reflective panelling was certainly a stealthy advantage. Through the window he was currently looking out of, he saw not only the three remaining customised vessels he had commanded on the attack on Molly and Jaxx's ship, but he saw the Beresian ship itself, docked, undergoing repairs approximately a quarter of a mile down the shuttle bay.

"This could finally be the end. Our work is almost complete."

Slater turned and walked out of the chamber, the lights dimming behind him. However, as he left, he began thinking to himself, that he could very well be too late. If the Resurrection project was indeed ready to action, the future could once again be in jeopardy.

RESURRECTION

TWENTY-FIVE

The nebula was beautiful. Never before had Molly seen such an array of colour in one place. Swirls of violet and indigo, were penetrated by bright pinks, and flashes of fiery orange. As she navigated the stolen ship between the energy currents, they flashed turquoise like bright, bold lightning strikes. A brief shudder reminded her that she was getting too close, and she adjusted course. Despite everything she had done to reach this point, she missed Jaxx. Not only his piloting skills, but his company. She had felt something very deep for him, and it had taken all of her strength to pull that trigger. A tear began to form in her left eye as she thought about him, but she quickly blinked it away, and reminded herself of her task.

She had made a copy of the map from the computer chip as soon as she had taken it from Finbar during their confrontation in the bar all those weeks ago. She knew Torath was not on board the *Challenger*. He had left her notes when she was teleported away suggesting he had successfully cloned a test subject, his brother. She therefore determined that he would probably have done the same to himself, in order to create a decoy. The project was too important to him. She had poured through all of his personal logs, and come to feel as if she really did know him. She had developed a debt of conscience to him. He had rescued her, and it had given her a chance to correct the mistakes she had made. The weapons development program had caused her planet to be destroyed, and Torath could help her fix that.

Another shudder to starboard, and another course correction. Sensors were picking up nothing, due to the intense interference. And then she saw it with her own eyes. A clearing in the rainbow array of mists and fogs. Faint, but discernible, no mistaking it. As she piloted the ship closer, her heart began to beat harder and faster. She found herself becoming anxious. She had sought this out for nearly eight years, and suffered so much in the process. And done things that she couldn't take back. When she thought of the number of lives she had taken, she felt sick, but she had been given no choice. Humanity must rise again.

She was now close enough to make out the markings on the hull. There were several scorch marks, and evidence of old hull breaches that had been repaired over the years. She was definitely in the right place. Sensors couldn't penetrate the hull of the *Trinity* due to a dampening field being emitted from the ship itself in addition to the nebula's own interference.

"Computer, open a channel to the *Trinity*."

"Unable to establish communication. There is no active communications array detectable on the indicated vessel."

That made sense. If Torath wanted to give the illusion of a ship adrift, then it would stand to reason he would have deactivated the array for ultimate radio silence.

"Computer, is there a docking hatch wide enough to accommodate this vessel?"

"Affirmative. The auxiliary port on the underside of the craft is large enough to accommodate this ship."

Molly altered her course, and changed her angle of approach to head for the docking port indicated by the computer. As the ship rotated one-hundred-eighty degrees, Molly fired the manoeuvring thrusters to position herself in line with the hatch, and carefully docked with the *Trinity* before disengaging her engines.

As excited as she was to finally set foot back on board the *Trinity*, she had been through enough tough scrapes to realise she needed to remain prepared for anything. She slipped her Saxon blade into her hip holster, and her largest disruptor rifle into her back holster. Clutching her handheld version, she tapped the decompression codes into the door panel, and with a whooshing sound, the door swung open.

Molly waited a moment, and became more anxious. The *Trinity* was in almost total darkness. A dim purple glow was all that could be seen down the corridor. As she cautiously entered the narrow space, the door closed behind her. Flipping on the light on the front of her disruptor, she slowly made her way down the hallway. The

199

ship was silent. Something didn't feel right. If there was truly any chance Torath was onboard, and the work had continued, then there should be some kind of evidence. The violet glow became brighter. Molly passed the sign for the cryogenics lab, and memories flowed back. Falling out of the broken tube, and being thrust into the firefight.

But as she rounded the corner, and the doors to the lab opened up, she was frozen in place. Standing before her, were twenty-five cryo-bays, one of which was empty. And off to the left of those was one individual bay, situated on it's own, with several tubes running from it, into the others.

Molly dropped her disruptor to the ground, and moved a hand to cover her mouth. She felt sick to her stomach. All thoughts and plans had gone out of the window.

For in every single tube, was an exact copy of Molly.

TWENTY-SIX

Molly sat on the floor, staring at herself, numerous times. How was this possible? Where did these copies of her come from? Where was the regeneration chamber? All she was seeing, was evidence of cloning. And more importantly, where was Torath? From further down the corridor, she heard a faint beeping. Forcing herself to turn away, she picked up her disruptor once more, and made her way down the corridor, almost feeling as if she was being watched, but by herself. It was a distinctly unsettling feeling, and one she soon hoped to shake.

The beeping was coming from a console on the bridge. As she made her way across, she could see the words **Incoming Transmission** displayed. Hesitant to see who was on the other side of the comm signal after what she had just come across in the cryo-lab, she forced herself to open the channel.

"Hello Molly."

The sight of Torath's pale blue face filled Molly with a sense of familiarity, and relief. Almost like that of a father returning after war. She could not form any words of reply, which caused Torath to smile, his hair turning a vibrant shade of red.

"It has been a long time, my friend. It is good to see you."

Molly nodded, wiping away tears.

"It's good to see you too, Torath."

The smile, however, soon faded from Torath's face and his tone took a darker shift, now the pleasantries were out of the way.

"Molly, I need you to listen to me, and do exactly what I say. I need you to disengage the *Trinity* from the cloaked moorings in the nebula, and pilot her on thrusters only to the coordinates I'm sending to you now. Do you understand?"

Molly didn't like the urgency he seemed to be displaying.

"Is there something wrong, Torath?"

"There is no time to explain now. Please just do as I ask and I will explain everything when you arrive."

And just like that, he cut the communication feed, and disappeared from the screen. The co-ordinates had appeared on the panel, and Molly laid the course into the controls. Most of the systems had come back online, triggered by Molly's arrival onboard the ship. But Torath was unsettled. Speed was clearly of the essence, so Molly disengaged the docking clamps to the stolen ship, and allowed it to drift away into one of the currents, where the lightning destroyed it within moments. With her hands now at the controls, she began to navigate the *Trinity* deeper into the nebula. Sensors were completely useless at this point, and her speed was limited not only by using just thrusters, but by the denseness of the nebula cloud itself, which was intensifying with each minute.

She couldn't help but glance back down the corridor as she made a course correction, towards the room full of her clones. She intended to get to the bottom of this when she saw Torath.

The cloud reached its highest level of density, and began impacting on the hull integrity. Molly attempted to redirect power from non vital systems in order to keep her on track, and the shields stabilised at sixty-one percent. The ship was still vibrating with the turbulence, and it reminded her of her last plane trip across the Atlantic on a visit to the United States. The guilt came rushing back in that moment, and she forced herself to focus again on her job of piloting the ship to its destination.

As the rocking and jolting of the ship reached a violent level, as fast as it had started, it ceased, the cloud density lifted completely, and Molly found herself in what she could only describe as the eye of the storm, at the heart of which, was an entire planet. A planet within a nebula. Nothing like this had ever been recorded before, at least not to her knowledge. The planet was a beautiful green and blue sphere, and the likeness to Earth could not be dismissed. The continents and the countries were obviously different, but the likeness was uncanny.

As the ship reached orbit, Molly felt the vessel jolt to a stop, and she was alerted that the remote piloting system had been engaged. As she watched on, the *Trinity* began its descent towards the planet surface. Minor turbulence rocked the ship, but nothing on the scale of the nebula cloud. It glided through the clouds, and as it penetrated the cloud cover, Molly raised her hands to her mouth in awe. She was now flying over a vast deep blue ocean. The waves rippled in the light cast down from the nebula cloud, creating a fiery sky, flashing and changing with the movement of the habitat above.

The ship began to slow, and Molly saw she was approaching a land mass. Below her, she watched as the *Trinity* passed over a sandy beach, surrounded with what looked like palm trees, and several kilometres of farm land, completely untouched. The ship began its final descent, and as it dipped down over the hills, a facility came into view, surrounded by what looked like a small city. Once the ship had finally landed, the cargo bay doors began to open, and Molly ran down the corridor, leaving her disruptor on the bridge, and flew out onto the ramp, not stopping until her feet were on solid ground. Standing there waiting to greet her, was Torath.

"Welcome home, Molly," he said, spreading his arms out wide.

As she ran in to hug him, he embraced her tightly, but only briefly, and soon released her, before turning and beginning to walk away.

"Follow me, time is of the essence."

Molly walked in step with her former rescuer, which was no mean feat for someone of his size.

"Torath, are we in danger?" she asked.

"It is a distinct possibility," he replied. "I have needed to make several excursions out of the nebula recently, and I fear my vapour trail is no longer dissipating effectively. Combined with that from the vessel you flew here, means I am certain we will be discovered very soon."

Molly had a new tinge of guilt. Had she inadvertently led others here?

"Torath… those women on the *Trinity*… they were… me."

Torath waved an arm as if to dismiss that statement out of hand.

"Those things are not important. The important thing is that you are here, and ready to help me in the final stages."

"Final stages?" she asked, tentatively.

Torath ignored her question, and led her into an extremely large laboratory, and paused. He turned to Molly, and gestured towards what was an enormous machine of biblical proportions. The machine was clearly fifty storeys high, and at least as wide as a city block. The vastness of the thing dwarfed that of any contraption she had seen before. Even the Beresian ship she and Jaxx had stolen, would be lost next to this thing. It appeared to contain several windows in many separate blocks, throughout the middle of the structure. In each window appeared to be cables, and a distinctive shape. A humanoid shape. At the top of the giant cylindrical structure, were massive coils of cables, and power cells, and wires all leading into the roof of the facility, and at either side at the bottom, were huge structural supports, each as thick as the *Trinity* herself.

"Is that…" she began.

"This is the culmination of the Resurrection project, Molly. Welcome to the regeneration chamber."

Her neck was beginning to ache from staring up at the machine for so long. She had always imagined a contraption the size of a cryo-pod, maybe the size of two or three, but nothing on this scale.

"Have you completed it?" she asked, almost afraid of the answer.

Torath smiled, and nodded.

"The programme and the directions have all been inputted, and they are ready to accept the DNA sequence. I'm glad you are back Molly. When you left here, I wasn't sure I'd see you again. Not after the last effort."

Molly's joy and excitement now shifted into uncertainty and confusion.

"Left here? I've never been here before. You sent me away when Lu'Thar attacked us, remember?"

Torath shifted uncomfortably, and began to walk away. Molly pursued him.

"Torath? Tell me what is going on here. And why were there clones of me on the *Trinity*?"

206

Torath stopped, and slowly turned to face her.

"Molly, those aren't clones of you. You are one of the clones."

An instinctive giggle escaped her lips, before her face turned serious once again.

"No, you're kidding. I'm… I'm me. I'm me!"

Torath sighed, much like you would with an impatient child.

"I sent you out three years ago to gather information, supplies, and to find your sister. Well, the other clone who went AWOL."

Molly was now on the verge of angry tears. She was trembling with emotion.

"No! No, you're wrong! I remember falling out of the cryo-pod, and you handing me the gun, and sending me away! I remember growing up on Earth, and I remember dealing with the Kaleys, and the Beresians, and the Deltarians!"

"None of that happened to you, specifically," replied Torath, again with a note of impatience. "The memories were implanted in you, along with a series of abilities drawn from the past of the original Molly. Her family were in the military, so I used her as a template for the regression technology, and managed to resurrect battle traits and abilities. Along with some fight schematics from the Saxon training academy, you were perfectly programmed to have abilities and knowledge beyond your experiences. Did you never wonder how you knew how to pilot different classes of ships, or martial

207

arts, or the history of different races? I programmed them into you."

Molly collapsed onto the floor, unable to process any of what she was being told. She was not the real Molly. She was four years old, and none of her experiences she remembered prior to that were her own.

"But everything that happened before the last three years?"

"Happened to the first clone. She was a magnificent piece of engineering, and the second phase of testing the technology. I had successfully resurrected traits from the past, now I had to try creating the body to match, so I decided to start with a clone. You see, the real Molly I rescued from Earth, she was never released from stasis. It was the first clone who fell from stasis during the attack. I didn't know this until afterwards when I returned to the *Trinity* to find her still encased in ice. Eventually, I met up with her again. Sadly it was on a trade mission with the Kaleys, and they handed over her body to me. Apparently, she was too weak for them. I implanted her memories into you, and altered them to provide a tale of triumphant escape."

Molly choked on fresh air.

"Triumphant escape?! Do you have any idea, how traumatised that experience has made me? Are you telling me, the guilt and tragedy, and hate I have for myself over Earth's destruction, the betrayals, the Kaleys, all of that was just *planted* inside me? What did you do to me?"

Torath snorted.

"Oh please, don't be such a drama queen. You survived, you're here. And now you get to help complete our mission!"

Molly instinctively reached for her blade. Grasping the handle tightly, she slowly withdrew it from her holster. Torath grinned at the sight of it.

"Ah, I remember that. I gave you, well the first you, your sister, that blade when I sent you on your way. Good times. I see you've both looked after it."

"Why? Why have you done this? If you have the original Molly, why do you need me?"

Torath began entering commands into his tablet, and movement began occurring within the chamber.

"I need you to keep the intruders at bay while I initiate the final programme, and begin the Resurrection project."

As he hit another command, at the heart of the chamber, in the largest window, stood the original Molly. Still wearing the clothes she had been rescued from Earth in, eyes still open, as they had been when the icing effect first took hold. On the ground, Molly looked up as if she was looking at a ghost, and yet whether it was something in her coding, or an instinctive reaction, but looking at this woman, she now knew that Torath was telling the truth, and she was not who she thought she was. She was a fake. A copy. A plaything for Torath to further his work.

"What happens to her when the process begins?" she asked through gritted teeth.

Torath gave her a cursory glance.

"She will have her DNA fully extracted, and sent into the chamber. That DNA will be stripped down to its base and the machine will extract the traits and traces of her ancestors. This will then be fed through the cloning chamber, and those individuals will be recreated in the separate chambers you see above."

"You didn't answer my question, Torath. What will happen to *her*?"

"She will be lost of course. But she will have provided so much more than she could have achieved on her own. The usable information contained within her genes will create over a thousand individuals from all points in her timeline. I can then replicate this with those members, going even further back, and bringing back more members of each family. The human race will be the first to be reborn! Her sacrifice will be worth it!"

Molly was horrified by what she was hearing. He was condoning the murder of an innocent woman in the name of science.

"You're going to kill her to further your experiment? Do you even care about the humans? Or is it the fact you can finally say to

210

what's left of the Saxon council that you were right? Fame, and glory, that's what you're craving!"

She began advancing on him, still gripping the blade tightly.

"What gives you the right to play God, Torath?!"

He began to back away at this point.

"You are the one who was so desperate to bring your people back, Molly. You're the one who has been racked with guilt over the destruction of your planet! You wanted this so desperately, that you've killed hundreds of people in pursuit of this! So what makes you any better?"

As Molly's rage exploded, and she launched towards Torath, blade raised, an almighty explosion rocked the facility, and both Molly and Torath were thrown to the floor, the blade cascading down the side of one of the chamber supports.

As she looked up, dust still clouding her vision, she saw a gigantic hole in the wall of the lab, and as she squinted to get a better vision, she saw the stern face of Jack Slater, and several of his crewmembers enter the building, weapons raised.

And standing just behind Slater was a familiar face. Albeit looking a little worse for wear, to Molly's disbelief, there stood Jaxx.

RESURRECTION

TWENTY-SEVEN

As Molly stood in her place and stared at her former companion, she couldn't help but notice, along with the visual marks and scars on his face and body, there seemed to be hidden ones. He seemed different, somehow. She understood that her immense betrayal of his trust would have an effect, but this was something else. Of course, she had not expected him to survive her attack. It had been an action she had not wanted to take, but did not regret it. There had been too much at stake. Even despite the treachery or Torath, she still had an immense desire to see this process through, and bring back humanity, by any means.

Jaxx spotted her, and for a brief moment, there was a flash in his already bright, pearl-like eyes. But a moment was all it was. Jaxx began to stride towards Molly, and as he did so, he extracted his new disruptor rifle, gave it a swift pump to load the fuel cell, and began firing purple blasts of energy towards her.

Molly launched herself out of the way, whilst in the background, Slater and his soldiers began charging their way towards the central computer console, their plans clear. They wanted to destroy the systems which controlled the chamber, and the chamber itself. Jaxx was not her priority. She needed to get away from him. There was only her and Torath against forty other armed assailants.

As she ducked and weaved her way around the metal railings surrounding the complex, Jaxx continued firing his shots. Several of them struck the railings and blew them away from their mountings, several chunks of metal, narrowly missing Molly, and falling down out of sight, between the deck plating. Jaxx had one thing on his mind, and that was to stop Molly and Torath with everything at his disposal. As he was being treated for his wounds on board the Decimator ship, Slater had brought him fully up to date with all of the events that had been shared between them, the Saxons, and since then, with the Deltarians. The information and evidence presented to him had changed him at his very core. He and his race had been engineered by humans, and he had learned about them as a child, and revered them, almost idolised them. But learning what they were to become, and that they were responsible for the destruction of all Valkor in the future, had hardened him in a very short space of time. He was now equally determined to destroy the technology as Molly was to save it.

From a gantry overhead, Torath had begun firing particle weapons, taking down several of Slaters men on their approach to the central computer, but his biggest trick was about to unveil itself. As he took cover, he opened up a panel on the adjacent wall, and began frantically typing in commands and security codes. Mini explosions rocked the gantry and its support beams, as Slater's men fired back, but the attack soon paused, as a klaxon bellowed around the entire facility, and the doors began to slam shut around the facility.

"Warning, intruder suppression systems have been manually activated. All exits have been sealed. Armed response has been authorised. Sterilisation of the facility will now commence."

From the tops of the walls, and the ceiling overhead, small turrets emerged, each with two barrels protruding from the main body, and each with an independent targeting sensor, directed by a red sight light mounted on the top. As the turrets began to power up, Molly took her advantage and took down the nearest man, snapping his neck instantly, and took his weapon, firing three shots towards Jaxx in quick succession. He managed to dive to his right and avoid the first two shots, but the third one struck him in his shoulder, and the sound of breaking bone was audible, even over the klaxons. As his shoulder shattered, Jaxx fell back, his immense height toppling him over the top of the railings, and as he disappeared out of sight, Molly began sprinting towards the central computer herself.

The weaponised turrets came to life in brutal fashion, swivelling with immense and deadly accuracy, firing five shots into each target. Slater's men were being dropped at a high rate, as high above them, Torath continued his sprint towards the top of the chamber, which still housed the original Molly.

Smoke and the sound of screams now filled the facility, as bullets tore through skin. Molly carefully made her way through the carnage, smoke obscuring her vision. She squinted, trying to see where she was going, grateful that the turrets were seemingly programmed to omit her and Torath from their attack patterns.

215

"AARGHH!"

A loud roar came from Jack Slater's mouth as he launched himself through the air, tackling Molly to the floor, both of them losing their weapons out of reach and out of sight, upon landing. The turrets had now wiped out all of Slater's men, and had lost their target lock on Slater himself, due to the clouds of smoke and his proximity to Molly.

"You will NOT succeed in activating that chamber! I will not allow it!"

Molly ducked down as a fist swung towards her left temple, and she delivered a swift upper cut to Slater's gut, causing him to drop down to one knee. As he did so, Molly backhanded him across his jaw, and he rolled onto his side to move away, blood casually dripping from the corner of his mouth.

"What are you even doing? We are all humans! We can save ourselves!"

Each person was trying to locate the other in the fog, from the sound of their voice, but quick movements were distorting the echoes.

"I've seen what happens when humanity is left unchecked in the galaxy, and it cannot be allowed to happen again. That's why we destroyed Earth. And that's why we will destroy this facility!"

Molly up until that point had not been aware that Slater had been the one to destroy Earth. She had suspected he was working with the Deltarians to track her down, and had spent time thinking he must have been part of a lost colony the Decimators had missed.

Her rage and anger grew within her to a level she had not yet felt. A new strength was growing within her, and the level of hate she now felt filled her very being from her boots to the tip of her head. Her fists balled up so tightly, her fingernails drew blood from her palms. Her ears began to siphon out the background noise, and she began to use her own voice to track him down in the mist.

"You? You destroyed Earth?"

A faint laugh somewhere off to her right.

"You mean Torath didn't tell you? He has no concerns other than furthering his scientific prowess. He doesn't care about humanity, he just wants to bring a race back from the dead. If he hadn't rescued you from the rubble of Earth, it would have been another species!"

A shuffle to the right, and the echo of Slater's voice sounded dead ahead.

"Tell me, Slater. Why didn't you end it all? Blow up your ships, take out the rest of you humans. If we are that dangerous, why are you still here?"

Another noise, this time to her left.

217

"We had to be sure. We had to make sure all humans were gone. Can't do that if you're dead."

She was definitely getting closer. She could almost see his outline as the fog began to clear.

"Let me ask you something, Slater. You claim you're trying to expel humanity from existence. Why don't you try and change it? Stop us from becoming what you say we become?"

Dead ahead, looking away from her, was Slater.

"Man cannot be changed, Molly. Humanity doesn't change. Have you ever looked at history? Four-hundred years of slavery, followed by hundreds of years of casual and institutionalised racism. Hundreds of years of destroying our planet with climate change, despite the warnings and knowledge of what we were doing. Always trying to go one step further, running before we can walk. Nothing changes."

Molly crouched down, tensed her body and sprinted at Slater, her footsteps being as light as she could manage, but still he heard her approach. He spun and prepared himself to strike back, but as Molly got to within six feet of him, a deafening boom struck the facility, shattering a section of the roof, and sending tonnes of metal, stone, and debris cascading from above, immediately followed by a direct energy blast into the facility, striking the ground between Molly and Slater, and propelling them thirty feet into the air in opposite directions, Slater being impacted against the

218

far wall, and Molly barrel rolling upon landing, sliding for five metres before finally coming to a stop, her ears ringing, head pounding, and a sharp pain in her left leg. As she glanced down at it, a piece of metal was protruding from her thigh, her trousers stained with a dark and sticky liquid. As the blood continued to seep out of her wound, she tore off her sleeve, and attempted to tie a tourniquet around the affected area. Pulling it tight, she uttered a loud scream, and preparing herself for the task, she gripped the piece of metal tightly. She braced, her breathing intensified, and she tore the metal from her leg in one swift pull, the lab consumed by her scream, echoing from every surface. She tore the second sleeve from her shirt, and this time tied it around the wound, but within seconds, it had darkened with her blood.

Through the now gaping hole in the roof, Torath watched as three Deltarian vessels circled above, launching attacks on the entire city.

"NO! STOP YOUR ATTACKS!"

Torath screamed at the air, as the Deltarian military continued their targeted destruction of the city that Torath had spent years constructing for the human population to live in. An alert sounded on Torath's wrist communicator, and he ran to the nearest terminal, activating the comm system. Lu'Thar's face appeared on the screen.

"Torath, it is done. Surrender now. You have lost."

"NEVER! I will not be defeated this close to success! Stand down Lu'Thar, or I will activate my secondary defences!"

"Within minutes we will have levelled your city and the facility. Your defences will be inoperable."

"We shall see about that, old friend!"

Torath terminated the transmission, and began to punch commands into the terminal with even more vengeance and fury than the last time. Despite the damage to the facility and the surrounding areas, the ground defences were still online.

"Perimeter defences activated. Please select targets."

More furiously inputted commands, before the computer responded.

"Targeting patterns accepted. Commencing program."

The vibrations and rumbling from the Deltarian attack was now joined by a bigger, much closer vibration as turrets began rising up from the ground. The Deltarian ships altered their firing pattern to target the devices, but they were fitted with some kind of adaptive shielding, and were unaffected, continuing to prepare to fire.

As Molly dragged herself to her feet, she saw Torath climbing down from a damaged platform above the chamber, making his way towards the secondary activation console. Fire now raged all around her, and with every blast from the Deltarians, more debris fell, the walls began to crack, and she knew that pretty soon, the power systems would fail on the chamber and the entire Resurrection project could be doomed.

220

Another blast from above, and the sound of metal creaking and twisting was audible, and as Molly looked up, the bolts holding the platform to the wall, sheared. The platform itself dropped from the wall, and swung down like a vine, and there was nothing Torath could do. As the floor vanished beneath him, his body plummeted downwards through the air.

As Molly watched, in shock, Torath's body slammed into the ground, sending a cloud of dust up from the floor.

RESURRECTION

TWENTY-EIGHT

"Captain, the ships on the surface are losing structural integrity. They are requesting reinforcements."

Lu'Thar has been watching from above the planet, somewhat reserved in his attack, as he was still grasping with the idea that he had been misled for over twenty years by someone he had considered a close friend. But now the time had come for him to make a final stand. Stop Torath, and the human woman, and destroy the regeneration chamber to prevent humanity from enslaving the galaxy.

"Ensign, take us down."

Fay'Lar gave him a glance which read 'are you sure?' to which he nodded and sat back down in his chair. Rather nervously, the helmsman took a deep breath, and laid his hands on the console.

"Yes, Sir. Beginning descent."

The enormous *Challenger* began slowly moving down through the outer atmosphere. The ship dwarfed those which had been sent to attack the compound, and as such, felt the effects of moving down through the atmospheric layers much more. The ship rocked violently, and warning signs were beeping all around the bridge.

"Captain? Outer hull temperature is increasing beyond safety limits. Structural integrity will soon be compromised!"

Fay'Lar held onto the arms of her chair tightly, as the turbulence increased.

"Time until we punch through?" she asked.

"Approximately thirty seconds, Commander."

"Redirect power from life support on the lower decks, and strengthen integrity fields."

"Aye, Commander."

Lu'Thar addressed his first officer.

"Commander, take the tactical station. I want all weapons online and available at a moments' notice."

Fay'Lar nodded, and moved her way back to her original post. The power distribution seemed to have worked, as the violent rocking motions thinned out, and as the crew watched, the *Challenger* penetrated the clouds, and began tapering towards the facility.

"Lieutenant Moltar, scan the compound. I want to know who is down there besides Torath."

"Captain, I think we have bigger problems."

"Explain?" asked Lu'Thar.

Before his Lieutenant had time to explain, the *Challenger* was battered by a barrage of weapons fire, and the science station exploded in a bright firework display of sparks and glass, sending Moltar cascading backwards onto the floor. As he came to rest, his face was unrecognisable with plasma burns, and no life remained within his body. Smoke poured down from the ceiling, and another series of hits caused the rear engineering stations to blow out one by one, sending officers scattering all over the place.

"REPORT!" screamed Lu'Thar.

A second officer made their way over to the destroyed science station, and burned onto the display was the sensor image of a large vessel. Three times the mass of the *Challenger*.

"Captain, it's a Decimator ship."

RESURRECTION

TWENTY-NINE

Molly was dragging her leg along the floor behind her. She was leaving a heavy trail of blood, having attempted to stand up and failed to support any weight. She was desperately trying not to look at the corpse of her former saviour. The impact of Torath's body on the floor had not been a pleasant sight. Warning sirens were now the latest sound to echo around the laboratory.

"Warning. Power supplies to the chamber are now at a critically low level. There is a significant danger of system failure."

The sound of the weapons fire outside was becoming louder and more frequent, and appeared to be coming from different sources, but Molly wasn't focussed on that. She had one goal, and one goal only. To activate that chamber and begin the resurrection of her race. But she was still twenty metres away from the control station. Her blood loss was now becoming critical, and her head was spinning. She fell flat to the floor, and her breathing was becoming more shallow. She began to drift between a conscious and unconscious state, and as she did so, she began to recall memories that she had never seen before.

Her usual nightmares of watching Earth die were once again playing out in front of her, but they were being interrupted by static which then revealed split second images. She saw a glass surface, a

227

cryo-tube. But she was looking at it from the inside. Another flash of the coldness of space spreading through her skin, and then she was looking at Torath, standing at a console, entering codes, and looking at bio-scans on a screen. The image was interrupted by the imagery of the river vanishing over the edge of a cliff, before she heard voices in her head. The sound of someone whispering instructions to her, and then another image of her looking to her left, whilst lying nude on a medical bed. She squinted and through blurred vision, saw multiple tubes containing multiple versions of herself. She was remembering her birth. Her birth as a clone. She shook her head, trying to dispel the imagery, but her head was still spinning with the loss of blood. Through the flashing images, and dream hallucinations, she could make out the console she had been striving to reach. Lying directly in front of her, was a discarded Decimator weapon, and a blinking light caught her eye, and as she strained her mind to focus on it, she saw it was coming from the main pod, containing the original Molly.

Fire and explosions were happening all around her, but she took deep breaths and mustered all of her remaining strength, and reached out her right hand. Gripping hold of the weapon, she focussed with all of her might, and she zeroed in on the main pod. Her breathing had slowed almost to a murmur, and as she took what she felt would be her last breath, she fired.

A brief beam of light left the end of the disruptor, and seemed to move through the air in incredible slow motion. As Molly watched,

228

her eyes slowly closed, and she fell back down onto the ground, just as the shot hit the locking mechanism on the main pod.

RESURRECTION

THIRTY

The beam above the Captain's chair broke free from the roof, and swung down from above, and as Lu'Thar dived out of the way, it smashed its way through his chair, before continuing on to destroy Fay'Lar's chair and finally falling to the floor. The bridge of the *Challenger* was in complete tatters. All the bridge crew were now dead except for Lu'Thar, Fay'Lar, who was now sporting a severe head wound, and the pilot, Ensign D'Kar.

"Captain, shielding is gone. Weapons are down to thirteen percent. We cannot survive much more of this."

Fay'Lar punched her weapons console which was now blinking on and off like a lightbulb. There was no response from anyone else on the ship as communications were down, and emergency bulkheads had sealed them in, so they were unable to receive medical attention, or to even make it to the escape pods.

Escape, however, was not on Lu'Thar's mind. He was a proud, and noble Deltarian. Any Captain who did not go down with his ship, was no Captain in the military.

"Ensign, status of the enemy vessel?"

Another explosion, and the front window on the bridge cracked, before another shot blew the front of the bridge out completely.

D'Kar was blown back out of his seat, and showered in glass, but quickly got up and returned to his seat.

"They are running on automation, Captain. There are no humans left on board, but their shielding is still at sixty percent, even with the modifications to the weapons we were given by the Saxons! And their weapons are at full power!"

"Fay'Lar, can we tell who is down there yet?" Lu'Thar bellowed.

"I'm reading… two humans… and two faint life signs I cannot distinguish."

"No Saxon life signs?"

Fay'Lar shook her head.

"Not unless it is one of the faint readings. However, Saxon bio-signs are one of the strongest to read, even near death."

Three or four blows came from the surface as the turrets continued their weaker level of fire compared to the behemoth that was the Decimator ship. As Lu'Thar looked down through the hole in the front of his bridge, he saw the last of his three assault ships destroyed. The level of bombardment had simply been too much.

"Ensign D'Kar, Commander Fay'Lar… you are ordered to abandon ship."

The two officers looked at him as if he had gone insane. For one thing, they were sealed in the bridge but for another, no true Deltarian soldier would abandon their post, let alone their Captain.

"Sir, with all due respect…" Fay'Lar began.

"Do not quote regulations or traditions to me Commander. You have a mission to complete."

Fay'Lar looked confused, but didn't have time to challenge the decision, before Lu'Thar spoke to the computer.

"Computer! Is programme Lu'Thar-Delta-Six still operable?"

A series of failing mechanical sounds came from the speakers above, before a muffled response was heard.

"Affirmative. Program is available, however, using it will result in total system failure. The ship will lose all power. Do you wish to proceed?"

Lu'Thar marched towards his Commander.

"Fay'Lar, you and D'Kar must shut down that facility. Find the human woman, and eliminate her. Do not let that technology become activated. Do you understand?"

Fay'Lar nodded, and she felt genuine sorrow for what was seemingly about to be the loss of her Captain. Another prompt from the computer came, requesting an answer. But Lu'Thar made two final gestures.

233

"As Captain of the Deltarian warship *Challenger*, and general of the Deltarian military, I hereby promote Ensign D'Kar to the rank of Lieutenant, and relinquish my rank of Captain to Commander Fay'Lar. You're Captain now, Fay'Lar. For Deltaria."

"For Deltaria, Sir."

The computer prompted again for an answer, and this time, D'Kar and Fay'Lar moved to stand beside each other, and Lu'Thar nodded at them both, before issuing his answer to the computer.

"Affirmative. Execute programme."

A beep of acknowledgement was audible and two individual teleport discs fired from the tactical console, and struck Fay'Lar and D'Kar on the back, before activating and sending them shooting upwards through the hull of the ship. Immediately following their departure, the ship lost all power, and fell as silent as the grave. Red lights illuminated the bridge, but there was no other form of active console or instrument. The Decimator ship seemed to sense the *Challenger* was now dead, and broke off its attack, descending back towards the surface. This was Lu'Thar's chance and he was going to take it.

He moved to the front of the bridge, and ripped the panel off the underneath of the navigation console, and immediately began tearing out wires. As the ship began to fall from the sky, Lu'Thar worked busily, until he could see the wiring leading to the now dead interface to the ships computer and its power source. Tearing

234

the cables out of the console, he reached for his disruptor, and began disassembling the weapon. The gravity was now becoming an issue, as the speed of the *Challenger's* descent was increasing, and the ship was falling at ever increasing angles, Lu'Thar struggled to hang on. As he removed the power cell from his weapon, he let the rest of the weapon go, and it bounced off the deck plating behind him, and out through the window. He jammed the power cell into a slot in the console, and reconnected the wires to the navigational array. It wouldn't give him much, but it would give him enough.

Struggling to hang on, he pulled himself up into the seat, and the console struggled itself into life. A message displayed on the screen warned Lu'Thar he had enough power for one manoeuvre. But one was all he needed.

"Computer, acknowledge."

"Navigational system operative. Estimated time until failure, fifty three seconds."

"Computer, target the Decimator vessel. Set a collision course."

RESURRECTION

236

THIRTY-ONE

"Hey… hey, wake up!"

The sound of someone's voice brought Molly back from the brink. Who was that? The voice was familiar.

"HEY! Come on! I can't get you out of here if you don't wake up! Wherever here is."

As Molly forced her eyes open, she found she was propped up against a wall, staring back at her own face.

"Okay! There you go, now I don't know how this is happening, but we need to get out of here right now!"

Original Molly put her arms around her clone and lifted her to her feet. But she resisted moving.

"No, you have to help me into the chamber."

Completely disorientated by her situation, the explosions, and the fact she was helping a battered version of herself to safety, real Molly tried to force the issue home that they really needed to leave.

"What? I just climbed out of whatever that is. We need to leave!"

"NO! If I don't get into that chamber, everything is lost! We're the only ones left! Now will you help me?"

Real Molly relinquished her stance, and still completely bewildered and overwhelmed by everything happening around her, she nodded, and the two of them began stumbling back towards the structure. As clone Molly glanced up through the roof, she saw a gigantic black ship moving towards them, firing at the turrets designed to defend the complex. As each turret was blown away, she squinted at the sight of a smaller vessel closing in on the larger one. She recognised it, almost immediately, even in her blood deprived state. And she saw what it was doing.

"GET DOWN!!!" she shouted.

As the *Challenger* struck the Decimator vessel, it carved its way through the top of the ship, and a cascade of heavy explosions tore its way down the spine of the craft like a knife, ripping it in half. Each half broke away from the other, and took two different paths. The debris remaining from the *Challenger* shot down to the ground like huge bullets, spearing the ground where they landed. One half of the Decimator ship impacted a good distance away from the facility, but the other half hit ground right outside, causing the ground to ripple like a wave, all the way along until the shockwave hit the walls of the facility. A crack shot up the external wall, and it split open like tissue paper.

As the two identical women watched on, the wall fell apart, and the debris crashed down around them, several pieces striking the supports holding the chamber upright, and the entire contraption

238

swayed. As the dust settled, the two women climbed back to their feet, and continued on to their destination.

"WAIT!"

A voice bellowed from behind them, laboured, but familiar. As they turned, they saw Jack Slater, drenched in blood, stumbling towards them, weapon pointed right at clone Molly.

"You shall not activate that device! You will…"

A flash of blue light from behind silenced Slater, and as his body fell to the floor, behind him stood two Deltarian soldiers. Clone Molly took this as a good time to speed up. They were only a couple of metres away from the secondary platform that led to the main chamber.

Fay'Lar and D'Kar sprinted towards them, but more debris began falling from above, and they were forced to take various diversions to avoid being crushed. Fay'Lar glanced through the open cavity in the laboratory and saw the wreckage of the *Challenger*. She took a deep breath, and thought once more of her Captain. But she was Captain now, and she had a mission to complete. The Decimator vessel had been on auto-defence, targeting anything in the vicinity, but now it was out of the way, nothing was going to stop them.

As Molly and her clone finally reached the chamber control panel, clone Molly began entering the startup sequence. Original Molly was looking around frantically, as the structure began to finally give way.

239

"Now what?" she asked.

Clone Molly, looked around, and then looked in real Molly's eyes.

"You need to leave."

"What do you mean leave? You just made me carry you all the way up here! I don't know where I am, or how you exist, or anything! I need to know what to do!"

"We don't have time for that, just go!"

Clone pulled a transparent computer module from the console and placed it into a memory slot. Entering commands, she downloaded all of the information from the computer banks onto it, and handed it over to Molly.

"Take this, and go. Please. Don't become what I did. Get away from here, and don't look back."

"I... I don't understand..."

"You don't need to. God knows, I didn't. But you're strong, and you'll get there."

A blast from a Deltarian disruptor struck the platform railings, as Fay'Lar closed in. Real Molly took the module.

"NOW GO!"

She took one last look at her clone, and turned, heading back down the platform. As she ran through a cavity in the wall, clone Molly turned and began inputting the final commands.

"Regeneration chamber ready. Please input final command code to begin."

The building was now raining down piece by piece, and behind her, Fay'Lar and D'Kar were now unable to pass the mounting debris. Fay'Lar opened up on her disruptor attempting to blast away the rock while D'Kar attempted to find a better position to fire at Molly, but neither were successful. Molly glanced down at the console, and entered the final code.

"Command code accepted. Execute the programme when ready."

Molly took a deep breath, and closed her eyes. As she went to hit the execute command, a searing pain shot through her chest. A gurgling sensation began to form in her throat and the taste of copper was overwhelming. As she looked down, the console was splattered with her blood, and protruding from her chest was a long Saxon blade. She could not catch her breath, and the blood in her throat was now pouring from her mouth.

As the blade was extracted, she collapsed forwards onto the console, and just managed to turn herself around. Tears welled in her eyes as she looked back at Jaxx. He held the blade downwards, Molly's blood still dripping from the tip. His eyes too, were filling with tears, as he dropped the blade. Molly struggled with her final

241

breaths, as her vision finally began to dissipate, and she slid onto the floor. And then she was still.

Jaxx stared at her lifeless body. He had been given no choice, but he felt as though he had run a dagger through his own heart. The building continued to collapse all around him, and he knew he had to leave, even though he didn't want to leave her lying there. As a huge block of concrete fell from the ceiling, it smashed through the main chamber, obliterating it, and landing on the command console, and beginning a cascade reaction.

As Jaxx watched on, one by one, the pods began to fall away from the structure, and crash to the ground. He knew it was time to go. He took one last look at Molly lying there on the floor, and turned away. Clutching his destroyed shoulder, he jumped from the platform, just as another section of wall folded in on it, burying that platform, and Molly along with it. As he ran, ahead of him, he saw Fay'Lar and D'Kar who had managed to work their way around the rubble, but the job was done. Jaxx waved at them with his good arm to run, and surveying the scene behind him, they obliged. The three of them jumped through a gap in the rubble, as the final parts of the building crashed down behind them.

242

THIRTY-TWO

As they lay on the grass, still trying to catch their breaths, Jaxx, Fay'Lar and D'Kar each thought back to how they had gotten here. Who they had lost along the way, and the sacrifices they had made. Jaxx in particular was a scarred individual. He had lost his home, his ship, his friends, and been forced to kill the woman he had begun to have feelings for. His torture at the hands of Jack Slater now seemed mild in comparison.

He had been lying on the scorched grass for two hours, in silence. Thinking about how Molly was prepared to murder however many people she needed to in order to bring back humanity. Jaxx had been shown by Slater, the effect that would have. He had even heard Slater telling Molly that exact same information. And yet, as Slater had suggested, it didn't change her mind. He so wanted to believe that his ancestors were capable of so much more. But now, he would never know. The humans were gone. The Decimators, and their ship was gone. And the technology to bring any of them back, was also lost.

"So what do we do now?" asked D'Kar, who unbeknown to the others, had been the first to stand up.

243

Fay'Lar looked at Jaxx, and neither of them had an answer. Fay'Lar glanced over her shoulder at the rubble, some of which belonged to her former ship. She stood up, and surveyed the scene.

"Well, Lieutenant. I'm a Captain without a ship. So my first suggestion, is we go and find one."

She held out a hand towards Jaxx.

"We could use a pilot, now D'Kar here has been promoted. What do you think, Valkor?"

Jaxx took her hand and she pulled him to his feet. He considered her offer, but he decided he wanted to be on his own for a while. That was how he had lived most of his life, and since he became involved with others, everything had turned sour.

"I appreciate the offer, but I'm going to take some time on my own."

Fay'Lar nodded in acceptance of his decision, and gestured to D'Kar that he should follow. She stopped momentarily, and looked back at Jaxx.

"If you ever need an ally in the Deltarian military, you know where we are."

Jaxx smiled, and nodded, and as Fay'Lar and D'Kar walked away, she spotted a small craft entering the atmosphere, heading out into the nebula.

244

"Who was that?" asked D'Kar.

Fay'Lar shrugged her shoulders.

"No idea, but hopefully, wherever that ship came from, there's another one."

The two continued on towards what they hoped was a hangar, leaving Jaxx alone. He kept wondering about the questions that were still unanswered. How did Torath manage to construct such a vast area on his own in such a short space of time? How did he manage to clone himself as a decoy for Lu'Thar, without him dying? After all, didn't he hear Torath telling Molly that the subject in the main chamber would be broken down into nothing? And more troubling of all, despite the evidence he was shown, if this group of people Slater called 'The Redemption' created the time travel technology, why did they not recreate it and come back in time to pursue them?

All of these questions were still unanswered, but taking a final look at the destruction laying before him, Jaxx couldn't help but think that all of them, however confusing, were now irrelevant. It was all over. He began his long walk towards the same proposed hangar that Fay'Lar and D'Kar had headed towards, albeit at a much slower pace.

The sun began to set above him as he walked out of view of the facility, but there was an extra glow beneath the rubble. Several chamber pods were visible, smashed to pieces, but below one of

245

them, in a gap in the rubble, was a flashing blue light. In the distance, a ship began to take off from the ground, sending a vibration through the soil for miles. As the vibration reached the rubble, several pieces of rock and concrete fell away to reveal a console screen, which portrayed a flashing message, and a display of a planetary system. The screen was cracked, and the display was losing power. The picture it showed was as clear as daylight. The image was of Deltaria, specifically the deepest point in one of the abandoned mine shafts. And the message itself glowed in bright red letters.

"Emergency procedure initiated. Secondary facility is now online."

THIRTY-THREE

Molly had taken in a significant amount of information in the last fifteen hours. Her mind was exhausted, and yet was running a mile a minute. She wasn't sure if her clone had known what was contained in that database or not, but she herself had not been prepared for the details it contained. She hadn't even had time to comprehend the fact that she was now two-hundred years into the future, let alone the series of events that had unfolded.

She was alone. Nobody to help. No humans. No Earth.

Don't become what I did.

Some of the last words her clone had uttered to her. What had she become? She had read about some of the experiences, as the database had shown Torath kept a very close eye on all of his clones, but to experience them? She couldn't even comprehend. Her clone had been forced to learn on the fly, and pick things up wherever she could, but she had also been pre-programmed with multiple self defence techniques and prior knowledge in her subconscious. The real Molly, didn't have any of that. All she had, was this very small shuttle craft, and one weapon, that she didn't even know how to use. She was grateful the computer was voice activated.

"Hello, um, Computer?"

A beep of acknowledgement.

"Erm… can you tell me where the nearest facility is for supplies?"

A brief pause.

"The nearest station is four and a half days away at maximum speed."

Molly looked around, and saw no obvious supplies available. Surviving four days in deep space with no experience would not be easy.

"Mr Computer, erm… are there any closer locations?"

"Negative."

"Are there any supplies on board this… ship? Food? Water?"

"This vessel contains emergency food rations and water supply for fourteen days, and a wide library of tutorials and video guides."

Molly let out a long sigh.

"Well I guess I'm going to be learning a lot while I travel."

The computer directed her to the location of the food, and was surprised when she opened the compartment to see that it was mostly Earth based food. As she reached for the mashed potato and gravy sachet, she sat back down in the only available seat.

"Computer, where did this ship come from?"

"This vessel was designed as an emergency evacuation craft to be used in the event of a global emergency."

"Who designed it?"

"This ship is of Saxon design."

"Saxons? The people that Torath was from? The man who saved me from Earth, and built the… the… resurrection building… chamber… thing?"

"Torath is a Saxon scientist. He constructed the facilities to house parts of the Resurrection project, including regeneration chambers, which suggested that it was possible to bring back a race of extinct beings, through reverse engineering of a subject host."

That was what Molly's clone had been trying to do, she realised. She was going to climb into the pod, and then bring back humans. But she suspected that her clone did not know as much as Molly now did. Having read the reports over the last day about Deltaria, the cloning process, and the invention of the Decimators, she wondered if she should go somewhere else, and worry about supplies later.

"Computer, where were the regeneration chambers located?"

"A facility is located inside of a previously uncharted nebula, on a purpose built planetoid, at the coordinates shown."

249

The display showed the nebula and planet that Molly had left in ruins just yesterday.

"The other chamber is located here."

The display now altered to show the same image of the Deltarian mine, shown on the display in the rubble.

"Computer, how far away is this location?"

"Approximately three days at current speed."

"Computer, take me there please."

THIRTY-FOUR

The mines of Deltaria were simply spectacular. Of course there were caverns, filled with darkness, and dust, and rock, and they were most certainly dangerous. But the walls were lined with precious minerals, and the same diamond-like substance which coated the skin of Deltaria's people.

This mine, however, was not so spectacular. It had been abandoned decades ago, after a tragic collapse which saw the loss of a young child, and was then closed off with no access permitted. At least, no access that Deltarians were aware of.

The base of the mine in question was over four thousand metres below the surface, and no natural light had ever reached this place before. Inside the rock face on the perimeter of the mine itself, was a slightly shaded version of the rock face that didn't quite seem to belong. On the other side of this cover, was a metal door, concealing a laboratory.

As the door was opened, the activity inside was frantic. There were only six Saxons inside, but each of them were running around, or typing in formulas into their consoles, and the pace was only increasing.

"Reyton, I need to see you please."

251

Reyton closed the door behind him, making sure to input the security lockout code, before sliding the artificial rock wall across it to conceal the entrance.

"What is it Podar?"

Podar was slightly shorter than his counterparts, and considerably younger. He was in fact one of the youngest Saxons left alive.

"We are having trouble with our guest. She was caught trying to open the seal on the regeneration chamber again this morning."

Reyton sighed. He had thought his troubles were now at an end, with the death of Torath, and the Decimators dead. And yet problems kept cropping up.

"Very well. I shall go and speak with her."

Podar stepped aside and Reyton walked through another doorway and down a long corridor, lined with rock on either side. They had been extremely careful when excavating this area, as this was where the collapse had taken place.

As Reyton approached yet another door, he tapped on the surface of the metal, before swinging the door open. Sat in the corner of the room, scribbling on paper, was a Deltarian woman, a young woman, no more than fifteen years of age.

"Now, my colleagues tell me you were trying to open the regeneration chamber again, Narlia. Is this true?"

The woman looked at him with fearful eyes.

"I just wanted to see what they look like. I've heard stories, but I've never seen one."

"Narlia, I promise you, when the time comes, you will learn all you need to know about the humans, but right now, we need to perfect the process. We can't have another Decimator situation on our hands. Goodness knows that was a mess."

"Do you think they'll be ready soon?"

Reyton smiled, and nodded his head.

"I think so. Hopefully this version of Mr Slater won't be quite so erratic."

Narlia smiled, before asking another question.

"Is there any word on my father?" she asked.

Reyton's facial expression changed to one of a more stern design.

"There is no trace of your father, Narlia. Or any other Deltarian. I'm afraid evidence suggests you are the only survivor."

The girl's eyes lowered to the floor, and she continued to scribble on her paper.

"I will leave you to your drawings. And please, no entering the chamber again, alright?"

She nodded, and Reyton left, closing and locking the door behind him.

Narlia continued to draw on her paper until she was finished. She smiled at the image, and stood up, walking it over to the softer rock. The wall was adorned with imagery from her childhood, or at least what she could remember of it. She pinned the new image up on the wall, alongside the others, and smiled again.

The image was of a Deltarian military commander, saluting his general. The name on the uniform of the commander was coloured in gold, with a black surround. Lu'Thar stood stern and proud in the picture, just as Narlia remembered him.

"I'll find you one day, father. I swear it."

THE STORY WILL CONTINUE...

R E S U R R E C T I O N

UNITY

- 2022 -

AFTERWORD

So brings an end to my first full length science fiction novel. I hope you enjoyed it, and are intrigued by what is to come. There is much more to come from this universe, and I have so many ideas for the story going forwards, and the plan is to write the second book, Unity, and release it in 2022.

However, as I am writing this, me and my wife Charlotte are expecting our first child, with the due date in February 2022. So as you can appreciate, the deadline will be subject to change.

In the meantime however, I will be continuing to work on my side project, Little Nightmares, which sees its second story released in a couple of weeks, details to follow.

It is my intention to write these short horror stories in between working on Resurrection 2 & 3, and release them on specific dates of the year. Then finally, when I have written and released all 13, then they will be compiled into one volume and released as the compendium, as originally intended.

Little Nightmares is something of a frustration for me, as it is inspired by the ideas that I didn't manage to squeeze into the Dark Corner series, and I can't get out of my head!

As I'm sure you can appreciate, the next twelve months are going to be incredibly busy for me, so please bear with me with regards to new content, updates, news and new releases, but I'm so excited to share with you news of what I have in the pipeline.

You can expect…

Another 11 entries in the Little Nightmares series over the next 2 years, including the next entry entitled 'Hungry Eyes'…

Two more chapters of Resurrection to complete the *initial* trilogy… yes that's right, I said initial. I don't intend to close the door on this universe!… I already have an idea for a fourth story!

A new chapter of my autobiographical entry, To The Moon & Back, detailing the build up and first year of being a parent…

…and!…

There are plans in the works, following popular demand, to potentially re-visit our favourite little town… that's right! Sometime in late 2023, I will be heading back to Wealdstone for a new one-off adventure!

So yeah, between having a kid, completing a couple of different series, and revisiting others, I'm gonna barely have time to sleep!

As always, I cannot thank all of my readers enough for everything they have given me, all around the world. Every month, I get sent a spreadsheet of my reader numbers, both as volumes and page count, and it never ceases to amaze me how many people all over the world are reading my books, and my stories. I'm writing this in November 2021, and just this month, I've had new readers through Kindle Unlimited in Japan! Amazing!

Of course, massive thanks must go to those who have never stopped supporting me and backing me, from my incredible wife, Charlotte, my parents Shirley & Vince, my sister and her family, my cousin Nicola, and my aunt and uncle Glen and Trev, my great-uncle-in-law and cousin-in-law (if that's a thing!) Richard and Nancy, and everybody else.

I keep going because of this support, and I keep writing because people keep reading it!

I also did an email interview with the people at KDP, in a question and answer style, much like a magazine interview, which I will be posting online fairly soon, to give you guys a little more insight into why I love writing the things I write.

So all that is left to say is thank you, again, and I can't wait for what is next to come into 2022 and beyond!

Dave.

AVAILABLE 20TH DEC 2021

LITTLE NIGHTMARES :

NOT SUITABLE FOR CHILDREN

Have you ever wondered if your toys come to life when you leave the room?

Sound familiar? Think again.

One family is about to discover this Christmas what happens when the toys say enough is enough, and decide to play with the family instead.

It's going to be a very red Christmas...

AVAILABLE AS AN E-BOOK EXCLUSIVE TO AMAZON

Printed in Poland
by Amazon Fulfillment
Poland Sp. z o.o., Wrocław
29 December 2022

4c9de22b-41bc-45ed-a226-fc71af52e805R01